'What Do Y[...]

Angie asked, her voic[...]

Ethan curled his index [...] then brushed his fingers gently over her mouth and up along her cheek. Her eyes fluttered closed for only a moment; then she remembered who this man was and what he stood for.

'What do you want?' she repeated.

Ethan took a deep breath and then went on. 'I want you to help me choose a date. One that's mutually agreeable to both of us. The sooner, the better.'

Angie shook her head slightly, hoping to shake off the buzzing noise that had begun to vibrate between her ears. 'A date? What are you talking about?'

'For our wedding,' Ethan told her.

'Our wedding,' Angie echoed incredulously. 'You're asking me to marry you?'

'Angel,' he said, his voice low and level and utterly serious, 'I'm going to make you an offer you can't refuse.'

Dear Reader,

Well, summer may be drawing to a close but don't worry, this month's selection from Desire™ is as sizzling hot as ever! There's lots of fun to be had too with mistaken identities, mix-ups and even a matchmaking comet to contend with!

Firstly, **Man of the Month**, Shane Nichols, gets himself in a muddle in Anne McAllister's *The Cowboy Steals a Lady*. He kidnaps his best friend's girl in order to stop her marrying another man—only he steals the wrong woman! And what a mix-up in Leandra Logan's *The Education of Jake Flynn*! Jake sends two very different presents to two sisters. But he's in for a surprise when the 'sensible' sister ends up with the sexy present.

Now to that comet: Elizabeth Bevarly starts her **Comet Fever** trilogy this month with *Bride of the Bad Boy*. Angie Ellison tries to blame a matchmaking comet for her attraction to the mysterious Ethan Zorn. Well, how *else* can she explain her shotgun wedding? Mattie Ryan, on the other hand, knows all the reasons for her marriage of convenience in Sara Orwig's *Her Torrid Temporary Marriage*. But what she can't explain is how things got quite so steamy!

Finally, Metsy Hingle kicks off her **Right Bride, Wrong Groom** series this month with *The Kidnapped Bride*. And in Carole Buck's *Three-Alarm Love* the question is whether this on-off couple will *ever* make it down the aisle!

Happy Reading

The Editors

Bride of the Bad Boy

ELIZABETH BEVARLY

SILHOUETTE
Desire®

*Silhouette, Silhouette Desire and Colophon
are registered trademarks of Harlequin Books S.A.,
used under licence.*

*First published in Great Britain 1998
Silhouette Books, Eton House, 18-24 Paradise Road,
Richmond, Surrey TW9 1SR*

© Elizabeth Bevarly 1998

ISBN 0 373 76124 4

22-9809

*Printed and bound in Spain
by Litografía Rosés S.A., Barcelona*

ELIZABETH BEVARLY

is a graduate of the University of Louisville and achieved her dream of writing full-time before she even turned thirty! At heart, she is also an avid traveller who once helped navigate a friend's thirty-five-foot sailboat across the Bermuda Triangle. 'I really love to travel,' says this self-avowed beach bum. 'To me, it's the best education a person can give to herself.' Her dream is to one day have her own sailboat, a beautifully renovated older model forty-two footer, and to enjoy the freedom and tranquillity seafaring can bring. Elizabeth likes to think she has a lot in common with the characters she creates, people who know love and life go hand in hand. And she's getting some first-hand experience with motherhood, as well—she and her husband welcomed their first-born, a son, three years ago.

Other novels by Elizabeth Bevarly

Silhouette Desire®   *Silhouette Special Edition®*

Silhouette Desire®	Silhouette Special Edition®
An Unsuitable Man for the Job	Destinations South
Jake's Christmas	Close Range
A Lawless Man	Donovan's Chance
*A Dad Like Daniel	Moriah's Mutiny
*The Perfect Father	Up Close
*Dr Daddy	Hired Hand
Father of the Brat	Return Engagement
Father of the Brood	
Father on the Brink	
†Roxy and the Rich Man	
†Lucy and the Loner	
†Georgia Meets Her Groom	

*From Here to Maternity
†The Family McCormick

For Lucille Akin, the bravest woman I know.

Prologue

"I think I see him."

"Where?"

"Up there. Just above the sycamore tree. About six inches to the left of the moon. See him?"

Fifteen-year-old Angie Ellison squinted hard and directed her gaze to the area of the night sky toward which her friend Rosemary March was pointing. All she saw was a big black smudge of darkness surrounding a silver sliver of moon, and a tiny little speck of white light that differed only marginally from the other stars in the sky.

"That little thing?" her other friend, Kirby Connaught asked incredulously. "That's Bob?"

Rosemary nodded. "That's him."

"That's nothing," Angie countered in a tone of disgust that most fifteen-year-old girls had mastered without problem. "Frankly, I'm not impressed. What's the big deal about Bob anyway? I mean he's just a big, gaseous fireball, right?"

Angie, Rosemary and Kirby lay on their backs staring up

at the sky, at the very back of Angie's expansive suburban backyard, where there were no lights from the town to mess with the comet's luminous glow. They formed an irregular, six-pointed star, the crowns of their heads touching at its center, their legs spread casually, their arms folded beneath their necks. It was 3:13 a.m., and they were waiting. Waiting to catch a glimpse of Bob.

Bob, or more specifically Comet Bob, was due to make his closest pass to the earth in the night skies above Endicott, Indiana, at precisely 3:17 a.m. For whatever reason, the comet returned to the planet like clockwork during the third week of every fifteenth September. And when it did, it always—*always*—made its closest pass at coordinates that were exactly—*exactly*—directly above the small town of Endicott.

It was an anomaly that many a scientist had tried without success to understand over generations, an enigma that brought them back like lemmings to the small, southern Indiana town every fifteen years—only to send them home again after Bob's appearance and disappearance, scratching their heads in wonder. And because no one had been able to explain exactly what caused Bob's regularity or his preference for Endicott, the comet's celebrity had grown and grown, and the little Indiana town had come to claim him as their own.

The September night was hot and surly in spite of the summer's end, and the scant breeze moving about the three girls' faces did little but stir up more hot air. Although school had begun three weeks ago, the appearance of Bob—absent since the year of the girls' births—and the subsequent Welcome Back, Bob Comet Festival for which Endicott, Indiana, became famous every decade and a half, called for a brief holiday. Schools were closed the following day, and all workers had been given an official holiday decreed by the mayor, just so everyone would have the opportunity to stay up late and get a good look at Bob.

But Bob seemed to have other plans this year. Although he was right on schedule, according to those with high-powered telescopes, unusually cloudy weather this year had kept him inaccessible to most casual observers so far. And the night was partly overcast, making identification of the comet even more iffy. Angie squinted harder toward the area the local astronomers had indicated would be Bob's stage, but she still saw nothing more impressive than a vague dot in the dark sky.

"I think somebody goofed," she said. "I don't think Bob is coming tonight."

"He'll be here," Kirby assured the others. "It's been fifteen years. He's never missed."

"Bob is already here," Rosemary insisted. "Up there above the sycamore tree, about six inches to the left of the moon. Look harder. It's not much, but I'm telling you, it's Bob."

Comet Bob actually had a much more formal name, but virtually no one could pronounce it correctly. He was named after an Eastern European scientist who had few vowels, and even fewer recognizable consonants, in his name, and who had been dead for more than two hundred years anyway, and the general consensus seemed to be, *What difference does it make?*

Comet Bob was Comet Bob, famous in his own right and for a variety of reasons. He was always on time, he was visible to the naked eye once he drew close enough to the planet, and Endicott, Indiana grew rich off his exploitation every fifteen years.

Oh, yes, and there were the legends, as well. Anyone who'd been around for more than one appearance of Bob knew full well that he was responsible for creating all kinds of mischief. Because of the dubious honor Endicott, Indiana claimed for repeatedly sitting smack-dab beneath the comet's closest pass to the earth, all sorts of local folklore had arisen over the years.

Some people said Bob caused cosmic disturbances that made the Endicotians—both native and transplanted—behave *very* strangely whenever he came around. Others thought Bob made people see the ghosts of their pasts. Then there were those who were certain that Bob was responsible for creating love relationships between people who would normally never give each other the time of day.

And, of course, there were the wishes.

It was widely believed by the townsfolk of Endicott that if someone in the small southern Indiana town was born in the year of the comet, and if that someone made a wish the year Bob returned, while the comet was making its pass directly overhead, then that someone's wish would come true the next time Bob made a visit. Angie had barely a passing interest in the legend of the wishes. But clearly, it was on Kirby's mind that night.

"Hey, do you guys believe that myth about the wishes?" she asked her friends.

"What?" Angie asked. "The one about them coming true if you're born in the year of the comet?"

"Uh-huh," Kirby replied. "Do you believe it?"

"Nah," Angie told her. "Wishes don't come true. Not by cosmic means or any other."

Evidently, Rosemary was inclined to agree. "Yeah, I don't think anyone in Endicott ever *really* got their wish."

"Mrs. Marx did," Kirby said. "She told me so. She was born in a year when Bob came around, and the next time he came by, she made a wish, and when she was thirty, when Bob came around a third time, her wish came true."

Angie and Rosemary turned their heads to gaze at Kirby, clearly interested in hearing more.

"What did she wish for?" Rosemary asked.

Kirby looked first at one friend and then the other. Finally, she confessed, "She wouldn't tell me."

Angie nodded knowledgeably. "That's what I figured."

"But she *swore* her wish came true."

Rosemary sniffed indignantly. "Yeah, I bet she did."

"She did," Kirby insisted. But when neither of the other girls commented further, she turned her gaze upward once more in an effort to locate the comet.

Angie did, too, noting that the nearly moonless sky was as black as she'd ever seen it, the almost utter darkness descending all the way down to the earth. Removed from the lights of civilization as the three girls were, they could scarcely see farther than each other's faces, and the scattered billions of stars above them seemed very far away indeed. Angie stared as hard as she could in search of Bob.

And she thought again about wishes.

"Well, we were all born in the year of the comet, right?" she said, taking up where Kirby had left off, turning to each of her friends. "So if you *did* make a wish, and if you *did* think it would come true in fifteen years, what would you wish for?"

A moment of silence fell upon the three friends, until Rosemary, always the most vocal, spoke up. "I wish that pizza-faced little twerp, Willis Random, would get what's coming to him someday."

Willis was Rosemary's lab partner in chemistry, the thirteen-year-old science whiz of the sophomore class, whose current focus in life seemed to be to make her life miserable. Rosemary had never much been one for scientific endeavors, and Willis had adopted a one-man—or rather, one-boy, as the case may be—campaign to belittle her and hold her in contempt for her egregious lack of understanding for his chosen field of study.

Angie nodded. The demand for Willis's downfall seemed a suitable wish. "How about you, Kirby?" she asked her other friend.

Kirby emitted a single, wistful sigh and turned her gaze upward again. "I wish…" she began softly. Her voice trailed off, and just as Angie was about to spur her again, she said, "I wish for true love. A forever-after kind of love. Like you read about in books and see in old movies."

Kirby's entire life consisted of going to school and caring for her invalid mother, Angie knew, with virtually no time left for anything social or enjoyable or steam letting. And most of the boys in Endicott just thought she was much too *nice* a girl to ever want to ask her out on a date. So the wish for someone to come along and make her life more romantic was in no way surprising.

"That kind of love doesn't exist," Rosemary told her.

"Yes, it does," Kirby objected.

"No," Rosemary replied immediately. "It doesn't."

"Yes," Kirby retorted just as quickly. "It does."

Knowing the two girls would argue all night if given the opportunity—Bob was making everyone in Endicott behave abnormally these days—Angie cut them both off by interrupting, "Maybe we'll find out in fifteen years."

"I doubt it," Rosemary muttered.

"How about you, Angie?" Kirby asked. "If you could wish for something, what would it be?"

"Yeah, what would you wish for?" Rosemary echoed, joining in.

"Me?" Angie asked thoughtfully. "I dunno. I guess I just wish something—or somebody—*exciting* would happen to this stupid town sometime."

"Riiiight," Rosemary said. "Something or someone exciting. No problem." She propped herself up on one elbow and turned to study her friend with a knowing expression. "Angie," she began patiently, "this is Endicott. *Nothing* exciting *ever* happens here. Even Bob can't work miracles."

"Well, that's what I wish anyway," Angie said.

"Fine. Hear that, Bob?" Rosemary shouted up to the sky. "My friend here, Angie Ellison, wants something or someone exciting to happen to Endicott the next time you come around. Write it down, will ya? Just so you don't forget."

And way up high, in the black night sky above Endicott, Indiana, Bob tilted and winked as he passed directly overhead. Then he began his departure from the earth to make his way toward the sun. He would be back, after all.

In exactly fifteen years.

One

Angie Ellison couldn't believe she was going to do what she was about to do. It was dangerous. It was immoral. It was illegal. It was downright wrong. But it was her only choice if she had any hope in the world of saving her father's livelihood, perhaps his very life.

She crouched behind a massive crepe myrtle that was still in full flower, scrubbed a finger under her nose to keep in the sneeze that threatened and stared up at Ethan Zorn's bedroom window. At least, she thought it was his bedroom window. She'd been in the house on only two occasions—first as a second grader on a field trip to what had then been a historic attraction known as the Stately Randall House, and again last week, when she'd been posing as a Junebug Cosmetics representative specifically so she could scope the place out.

On the first occasion, Ethan Zorn hadn't even been living in Endicott, Indiana, and his shadowy specter hadn't been a threat to Angie's family. On the second and much more recent occasion, the illustrious Mr. Zorn—who was now renting out what had become the Stately Randall Guest House once the Randalls had run through the Stately Randall Inheritance—hadn't been home.

Of course, she'd known he wouldn't be home when she'd lifted the big brass knocker on the front door. That would have interfered with her plan. Instead, she had opened her phony sample case for his housekeeper, had faked an upset stomach and had fled to the bathroom—where she'd managed to hack out some pretty convincing retching sounds, she recalled with some pride now.

The housekeeper had run to the kitchen for a glass of water and an antacid, and Angie had run upstairs to get a quick look around. And as best as she could remember, the window directly above the crepe myrtle *should* be the master bedroom. She was pretty sure it was, anyway. At least, she thought it was. In any case, she hoped it was, because that was where she was going in.

A damp blond curl escaped from the black baseball cap she'd crammed backward on her head, and she tried without success to blow back the unmanageable tress that plastered itself to her forehead. She was more than a little uncomfortable in the long-sleeved black T-shirt and jeans, with the heat of an extended summer breathing down her neck.

September in southern Indiana might as well have been July in the Amazon jungle, she thought. The air was oppressive, unruly and hot, and in no way conducive to breaking and entering. But she'd had to wear something to cover up her dark gold hair and ivory skin; otherwise she would have reflected the scant moonlight better than a mirror.

She rose quietly and began to make her way around the circumference of the big brick mansion, her black Reeboks whispering softly on the dry grass, her breathing thready and irregular. Belatedly, she realized there was probably an alarm system that she would have to contend with, then decided that no, people never even bothered to lock their doors in Endicott, because nothing ever happened here. Even big-time crooks like Ethan Zorn probably wouldn't worry about someone coming in uninvited. Those things just didn't happen in Endicott.

Not even to mobsters.

So Angie decided her chances were fifty-fifty that she would be successful in her first, and without question last, attempt at tangling simultaneously with the law and the criminal element. All in all, they weren't bad odds, she decided. They were certainly better than the ones that awaited her if she didn't succeed in her quest. Because if she couldn't uncover proof that Ethan Zorn was the low-life scumbag, murdering slug she knew him to be, then her family could lose everything.

As she drew near an open window, she heard the sound of music tumbling from inside—The Brandenburg *concerti*. Having minored in music, she would have recognized the lush, raucous compositions anywhere. Of course, such studies hadn't helped Angie further her career in journalism. She was, after all, still working for the *Endicott Examiner*. And even at that, she still hadn't won a front-page byline. Not that working the crime beat was so bad. She had wanted to be a crime reporter, after all. She just wished there were some crime in Endicott to report. It would make her job infinitely more interesting.

Not for the first time, she hoped that her escapade tonight, in addition to helping out her family, might result in a really, really good story, too. And then the *Examiner*'s editor, Marlene, would have to reward Angie's journalistic integrity and spunk. Maybe the story would even be syndicated, she thought further, fairly drooling over the fantasy. She could already see her name on the front page of the *New York Times*.

Of course, then mobsters everywhere would know where to find her. She frowned at the realization for a moment, wondering yet again if she was doing the right thing. Then the music ended abruptly, and she had no more time to think. She hurled herself against the cool brick building behind her, flattening herself against the wall, fading into a shadow. She told herself not to panic—Ethan Zorn was still out of town. She knew that, because she'd called her friend Rosemary, who worked as a travel agent—and who owed Angie more favors than she would ever be able to repay—to find out his itinerary. So it must have been the housekeeper who had switched off the concert.

Angie braved a quick dip of her head toward the window, gazed into a room furnished in Early Conspicuous Consumption, and saw that it was indeed the white-haired, mild-mannered Mrs. MacNamara who was fiddling with the stereo dials. And she kept fiddling for a good three minutes until she located the alternative station operated by the local high-school communications class. Only when the *boom-boom-boom* of Nine Inch Nails slammed against the walls did Mrs. Mac-Namara move to a chair by the grand piano and pick up her knitting.

It's that damned comet, Angie thought, shaking her head in wonder. It would be passing directly above Endicott in a week and a half, and everyone always said it made people do things they'd normally never do.

Like break into a house one had no business breaking into, she thought further, dropping to her hands and knees to crawl beneath the open window. Like risk the wrath of a malevolent killer like Ethan Zorn to keep her family safe.

Actually, Angie didn't know for sure that Ethan Zorn had ever killed anyone. She simply assumed that he had, given his line of work. Mobsters were always killing people, weren't they? Or at least they were hiring assassins or others of such ilk to do the killing. Until recently, there had never been any mob activity in Endicott. Not until Mr. Zorn had come to town. But now there was all kinds of talk of illegal goings-on. Well, some talk anyway. A little. Angie just wished she could pin down exactly what those illegal goings-on were. She was the crime reporter, after all.

She moved around the perimeter of the house in silence, and when she was satisfied that Mrs. MacNamara was in fact the only person home, Angie made her way back to the area below the alleged master bedroom window. Two stories hadn't seemed all that high in broad daylight. But now as she squinted into the darkness above her, that window seemed a pretty fair climb.

She filled her lungs with the hot September night and released the breath slowly. There was nothing else for it—she had no choice. Besides, the waterspout was so conveniently located at that corner of the building—and directly beside Ethan Zorn's bedroom window—that she just couldn't resist.

Gripping the metal spout firmly with one black leather-gloved hand, Angie dug the toe of her black high-top sneaker into the wide space between the bricks and heaved herself upward. Slowly, steadily, clawing first the bricks and then the drainspout, she made her way up the side of the building, feeling oddly exhilarated, like some nuclear-age superhero in a garishly painted comic book.

It wasn't until she reached the bedroom window that Angie began to panic. Because she realized then that deep down in her heart, she had been hoping the window would be locked and impassive, so that she could scrap this whole silly plan and go home for a good, long, helpless cry. Unfortunately for her, though, the window was not only unlocked, but open wide to allow in the warm, early-autumn breeze. It was going to be a piece of cake to break into Ethan Zorn's house.

Dammit.

With one final, heartfelt sigh, she reached for the concrete windowsill and swung her body toward it. For a single, brief moment, she hung there by both hands, berating herself yet again for doing something so incredibly stupid. Then she inhaled a deep breath, pulled herself upward and rolled herself over the sill and into the house.

Ethan Zorn rolled his itty-bitty, outrageously expensive car to a halt in front of his rented house and swore yet again that he would never, ever, not even if his life depended on it, fly standby again. It was too stressful, too unpredictable, too plebeian and too crowded.

Of course, he reminded himself, there had been a time in his life when he'd loved crowds and unpredictability, not to

mention acting plebeian. But he'd never much cared for stress.
Funny, how over the last decade he'd managed to completely
banish from his life the things he had always loved, and nur-
ture the one thing he had always hated. Or maybe it wasn't
so funny after all, he thought further with a frown. Certainly,
it hadn't been fun.

He pushed the troubling thoughts away as he shoved his car
door open. Then he unfolded himself from inside, arched his
body into a long, lusty stretch on the pavement and reached
back toward the passenger seat for his briefcase and garment
bag. The two items seemed to be his constant companions
these days, and he noted absently that both were starting to
show signs of fatigue and wear.

Much the way he was himself, he ruminated almost whim-
sically. But then, in his line of work, men like him never lasted
long.

After kicking the car door closed with his heel, Ethan ac-
tivated the alarm, wondering why he bothered. His newly
adopted headquarters—he hesitated to consider the small town
of Endicott, Indiana his home—was a place rife with decency
and wholesomeness, more's the pity. But he was accustomed
to watching his back in all areas of his life, and wasn't about
to stop now.

His house keys jangled lightly as he ascended the steps and
crossed the wide porch, and as an afterthought, before insert-
ing the key into the lock, Ethan tried the front door. Unlocked.
Again. He was going to have to have yet another chat with
his housekeeper, Mrs. MacNamara.

Of course, Mrs. Mack had grown up in Endicott, so she
couldn't possibly understand what dangerous elements existed
out there in the big, bad world. Endicott was the heart and
soul of midwestern America, a place where dreams and wishes
actually still had the potential to come true.

It was almost laughable, really, Ethan thought, the naïveté
and blissful ignorance of this town. If people had any idea
what he was really doing here, they'd pack up their children
and pets and run screaming for the safety of the shallow green

hills outside town. Fortunately for Ethan, he'd covered his tracks well. But then, that was absolutely essential in his line of work. One misstep, and he could be dead.

The front door creaked comfortably as Ethan opened it, and he was assaulted by the unlikely percussion of hard-rock music. Following it to the sitting room, he saw Mrs. Mack sound asleep in a chair beneath her knitting, and the stereo speakers fairly dancing on the bookshelf with every *thumpa-thumpa-thumpa* of a bass guitar. He crossed to the receiver and switched it off, and glorious silence descended to awaken the elderly woman.

She blinked at the soft light enveloping her like a shawl and met Ethan's gaze. "Oh. Mr. Zorn. You're home early. I wasn't expecting you back until tomorrow night."

Ethan swiped a hand wearily over his face and rubbed his forehead hard. "My business concluded earlier than I thought it would, so I went ahead and came back. Everything okay?"

His housekeeper nodded. "As well as can be expected with Bob on the horizon."

He shook his head. So she had been sucked in by all that comet garbage, too, he mused. That was the only thing about this town that Ethan found disturbing. This comet hysteria that seemed to have been affecting everyone since the day he'd arrived a couple of weeks ago. Comet Bob had been blamed for everything from missing pets to power outages to slow mail delivery. And every time local citizens did something stupid—whether it was speeding right by a traffic cop or getting caught in the act by one's spouse—they conveniently blamed it on Bob.

"Fine," Ethan said, dismissing the comet talk before it could begin. Suddenly, he was too tired to berate his housekeeper about the front door, so he ran a big hand wearily through his black hair and told her, "I'll just turn in, then."

Mrs. MacNamara nodded again. "Me, too. Ever since Bob was first spotted out there last month, I've been completely sapped of energy."

Of course, Ethan thought, that would have nothing to do

with the fact that the woman was nearly eighty years old and had recently taken on the total responsibility for her fourteen-year-old great-grandson, who was, if nothing else, a juvenile delinquent. No way could it be that. It must be Bob who was responsible for her sudden weariness.

"You do that, Mrs. Mack," he said, keeping his thoughts to himself.

He waited until his housekeeper was out of sight, then shrugged out of his Brioni suit jacket and tossed it over his arm, rolling his shoulders against the pressure of the holster strapped across his back. The big MAC-10 pistol tucked inside had traveled in pieces from Philadelphia in the overstuffed garment bag Ethan had checked for the flight. But the moment he'd collected the bag from the luggage carousel, he had ducked into the nearest men's room to quickly reassemble it, fastening the gun back in place. He felt far too vulnerable without it.

After loosening his Valentino necktie until it hung unfettered beneath his collar, Ethan hoisted his garment bag over his shoulder, gripped his briefcase more firmly and headed upstairs to his room. As he silently ascended the plushly carpeted steps, he switched his briefcase to his other hand and began unfastening the buttons on his Versace dress shirt, pulling it free of his trousers.

Comfort. That was all he wanted at the moment—comfort and relaxation. He paused outside his bedroom door to toe off his Gucci loafers, and was about to reach into the room to switch on the light, when he heard a strange, soft sound whisper through the darkness on the other side. The squeak of a bedspring, he realized immediately. Someone was in his room, squeaking his bedsprings, no less.

He took a single, silent step backward and lowered his burdens to the floor without a sound. Then he plucked the MAC-10 from his holster and flicked off the safety. The balmy night was suddenly suffocating, and he swiped at a thin sheen of perspiration that dampened his upper lip. Then he stepped toward the bedroom door again, pressed his hand flat against the wall and reached around to flick on the light switch.

As the bulb burst into bright white light overhead, Ethan moved into the doorway with his gun drawn before himself, his legs braced, with feet planted firmly against each side of the doorjamb. He had expected to see any number of people greeting him just as menacingly on the other side.

What he *didn't* expect to see was a petite blonde dressed completely in black, standing on tiptoe at the head of his bed with the pillows piled beneath her feet, a position that *almost* gave her the additional leverage needed to reach the painting of Moby Dick overhead. She spun around at the intrusion of light and promptly lost her footing, falling hard on her fanny at the center of the mattress.

When she saw Ethan's menacing stance behind the big, black gun, she gasped and slapped both gloved hands over her mouth, as if she were trying to stifle a scream. Her dark eyes widened in terror, but she uttered no further sound. Her body seemed to tremble all over, and her chest rose and fell erratically as she struggled to take in enough breath.

Instinctively, Ethan knew that she had broken into his house for some reason other than harming him physically. What on earth that reason could possibly be, however, had him totally mystified. Although he'd been living in Endicott for two weeks now, he couldn't recall ever having seen the woman who had invaded his house. Because he definitely would have remembered a woman like that. Not to mention eyes like those.

A brown-eyed blonde, he marveled. He'd always had a *major* thing for brown-eyed blondes. How very fortunate to find one in his bed now.

When he realized how frightened she was of him, he knew he had the upper hand, and he was helpless to prevent the smile that curled his lips. Tightening his grip on the gun, just to make her even more frightened—and therefore more amenable to answering his questions—Ethan took a few steps into his room, kicked the door closed behind him and reached quickly back to twist the key in the lock. Then he withdrew the key and tossed it carelessly to the other side of the room.

Still cupping her hands tightly over her mouth, the woman watched the slim length of metal arc delicately into the air, and took note of its descent and landing behind the Queen Anne chair in the corner by the fireplace. Her gaze moved from there to the open window opposite the bed, and Ethan could see that she was already weighing her chances with both escape routes, wondering which might provide the best alternative.

Nice try, he thought. He wasn't about to let her get away that easily. Maybe not at all.

He took a few more steps toward the bed, the slight movement enough to bring the woman's head whipping back around, her gaze locked on his. She finally dropped her hands from her mouth, but she still seemed unwilling—or unable—to make a sound. And she still didn't make a move from the bed.

As Ethan drew nearer, he realized she was even smaller than he'd originally estimated, and he wondered what the hell she thought she was doing breaking into the home of a man twice her size and weight. She must love to live dangerously, he decided. So danger was exactly what he would give her.

She remained motionless as he completed his approach, and he had to force himself to stop at the edge of the mattress and not crawl into bed beside her. Instead, he fastened his gaze to the black baseball cap that sat backward on her head, and the spray of loosely curled dark gold hair springing from the opening that normally would have been in the back. Then, as salaciously as he could, he skimmed his gaze downward, meeting her eyes levelly before turning his attention to her mouth, her breasts, her body.

"Well, well, well," he said softly after completing his inventory. When the woman edged backward to press herself against the headboard, he broadened his smile to bare his teeth, held his gun level and perched on the edge of the mattress.

"Who's been sleeping in my bed?" he wondered aloud. "And, more important than that, why is she still here?"

Hoo, boy, Angie thought with only a vague sense of reality. She was in it now. Deep. As she met the gaze of the big, lethal-looking man who had caught her searching his bedroom—because it was way preferable to staring down the muzzle of the big, lethal-looking gun he had trained between her breasts—she wondered what exactly she was going to do now.

Thinking back, she supposed it might have been a good idea to plan an escape route in case Ethan Zorn discovered her presence in his home. But at the time, being discovered just hadn't seemed likely. And besides, at the time, she'd been too busy trying to decide what to wear.

Hindsight's twenty-twenty, she thought now.

She supposed, if she tried really, really hard, she could convince herself that the menacing Mr. Zorn wasn't planning to shoot her. Otherwise, he probably wouldn't have locked the door and thrown away the key—it would only hinder him in the speedy disposal of her body. Not to mention the fact that if he had planned to shoot her, he probably would have pulled the trigger by now. So maybe all this business with the gun was just a little something he did to scare people.

As far as Angie was concerned, it worked.

"You're not going to tie me up, are you?"

The question was out of her mouth before she even realized she was thinking it. She squeezed her eyes shut tight. Idiot, idiot, idiot, she berated herself. Why on earth had she asked him such a thing?

When she opened her eyes again, Ethan Zorn was gazing at her with one eyebrow arched in speculation, as if he would like very much to take her up on her offer.

"Do you *want* me to tie you up?"

Instead of saying anything else that might make her sound as stupid as she felt, Angie clenched her teeth together hard, to keep her mouth firmly shut. Then she drew in a deep breath and held it, and waited to see what he would do.

"I guess I could scare up some rope from *somewhere* in the house." He smiled. "If it means that much to you. Then again," he added, his smile growing lascivious, "maybe you'd like it better if I used some of my neckties. They're silk, you know. Much less likely to leave marks."

Still Angie only continued to stare at him, unable to make a sound.

"Well, maybe some other time," he said, clearly sorry she hadn't responded more enthusiastically. He eyed her more intently. "So if you're not here looking for some cheap thrills—which, incidentally, I'd be happy to provide—then what are you doing in my bedroom?"

Angie didn't—couldn't—say anything in response.

"Well?" he asked.

She bit her lip and finally managed to find her voice. It was barely a squeak, granted, but at least she was able to chirp, "Well, what?"

He waggled the gun a little, a silent indication that he thought she should already know what he was talking about.

Angie scrunched up her shoulders and pretended not to understand, hoping for some kind of divine inspiration or medical intervention to offer an opportunity for escape. She was working on a good heart attack as it was. Maybe, if she could just buy herself a few more minutes, it would become a full-fledged coronary arrest, and she'd be saved the messy outcome of a shooting death.

Ethan Zorn eyed her curiously. "I'm waiting for an explanation, Goldilocks." His voice was low and level and redolent of the blue-collar accent one found so prevalent in the northeastern part of the country. "What are you doing in my house?" he added. "My bed? Your porridge been kind of cold lately? You looking to warm things up a bit?"

For one very brief instant, it occurred to Angie that Ethan Zorn had the most beautiful, bottomless, benevolent brown eyes she'd ever seen. Like Bambi's mother. Or even Bambi himself. Then she shook the sensation off and reminded herself he was a killer. Well, probably a killer, anyway. And killers didn't have benevolent Bambi brown eyes.

"Oh, is this *your* house?" she asked, feigning surprise, still hoping to buy herself some time.

He didn't look anywhere at all convinced by her phony confusion. "It's one my employer is renting for me while I have business here, yeah," he told her.

She glanced quickly around at her surroundings, pretending to see them for the first time, then smacked her palm soundly against her forehead. "Oh, wow, am I embarrassed. I thought this was Bumper Shaugnessy's house. You know Bumper, of course, don't you?"

Ethan Zorn continued to study her through narrowed eyes, and didn't respond at first. Angie kept silent, though, thinking every minute she could stall would bring her one step further away from winding up a tidbit in the *Examiner*'s obits later in the week.

"Uh, no," Zorn finally said. "Can't say as I've made Bumper's acquaintance."

She pretended to be amazed. "But *everyone* in Endicott knows Bumper. Ever since that incident with the Indiana Corn Queen at the Madison County Fair. Now, surely you heard about *that*."

Again the big man sitting on the bed beside her narrowed his eyes at her. "Um, no, sorry. Missed that one, too."

Angie waved her hand spiritedly. "Oh, this is a *great* story. You're gonna love it. See, what happened was that Boomer was actually dating Dierdre's twin sister, Daphne—Dierdre being the Indiana Corn Queen, of course—and he didn't real-ize—"

"Who *are* you?"

Angie blinked quickly, and once again found herself pinned to the spot by Ethan Zorn's espresso gaze. "I'm Angie," she replied automatically, wondering when she had chosen to speak. "Angie Ellison."

He shook his head, clearly confused. "Why are you in my

house? In the dark? Dressed in black? As if you were trying to…oh, say…rob the place?"

Once more, she shook off the odd sensation that the man sitting beside her—the man holding a gun on her, the man who was a threat to her entire family—was really just a cream puff deep down inside.

"I told you," she said softly, forcing the words out of a mouth suddenly gone dry. "I thought this was Bumper Shaugnessy's house."

Ethan Zorn shook his head. "Uh-uh. No way, sweetheart. I ain't buyin' it."

In one swift, deft move, he pointed the gun toward the ceiling, ejected its clip with a loud *ka-thwack,* checked it and tucked it back into the grip. Then, when the cacophony of scraping metal fell silent, he trained the ugly weapon on Angie once more.

"Now, then," he said. "Let's try this again. Who are you, and what are you doing in my house?"

"I'm Angie," she repeated. "Angie Elli—"

"I got the name down fine the first time, honey. I just don't recognize it." He dropped his gaze briefly to her mouth, then brought it quickly back up to her eyes. "Help me out here, or I'm going to have to resort to doing something I don't wanna have to do."

She inhaled a deep breath and scrambled for something that might explain her presence in a halfway plausible fashion. "Um…would you believe I'm…uh…delivering some Junebug cosmetics that your housekeeper ordered last week?"

Ethan Zorn shook his head very slowly. "No, I don't think I believe that. Try again."

Angie bit her lip. "Um…would you believe I'm working for 'Bugs' Burger's Extermination—at 'Bugs,' we think the only good bug is a dead bug—and have reason to believe that a rare breed of night-crawling *cucaracha* is infesting your walls?"

Again, that slow shake of his head. "Nope."

Angie gave it one last shot. "Would you believe, um…that

I've been admiring you from afar for some time now and just wanted to make your acquaintance?''

That, at least, brought forth a smile from the inimitable Mr. Zorn. Unfortunately, it was a decidedly lascivious smile, and Angie began to think maybe that last attempt at explanation might not have been such a good idea after all.

''Although I think I like the idea of being…admired from afar,'' he began, ''something tells me that's just not quite it, either. Three strikes, Goldilocks,'' he added, lifting the gun that had begun to droop. ''Unless you wanna give it one last shot—no pun intended—and tell me the truth this time, then you're outta there.''

Two

Ethan Zorn had been in the business a long time, and he'd met more than his fair share of characters along the way. Manny "The Meat Hook" Moran, for instance, came quickly to mind. And Two-Fingers Nick. Joey the Knife. Goosey Lucy…or something like that—Ethan could never quite remember that guy's name. And then there was that South Philly boy whose name had always come out sounding like "Lenny Bagagroceries."

But he'd never encountered anyone quite like Angie Ellison. Angie "The Angel" Ellison, he decided. Somehow, the name fit her. There was something about her that reeked of a higher existence, a higher standard. In addition to being beautiful in a way that Ethan could only describe as *ethereal*—yeah, that was a good word for it—there was an innocence and beatitude about her that was unmistakable. And although just about everyone in this hick town seemed naive to a fault, on this woman, it was carried to new heights.

He just wished he knew who the hell she was and what the hell she was up to.

She should be terrified of him, he told himself. He was twice her size, armed, and she was locked in a bedroom with him. For all she knew, he intended to kill her. Any other woman would have been scared speechless. But Angie Ellison was actually flirting with him. *Flirting,* for God's sake. That was the only way Ethan could interpret the look on her face, the timbre of her voice, the playfulness behind her words. Yeah, she was trying to save her life—it didn't take a genius to figure that out. But she was doing it so…so…lightheartedly.

It was giving him the creeps.

Okay, so maybe he could ascribe her relative easiness at being made a hostage to the fact that she was obviously a native of Endicott. One thing Ethan had learned since locating here, the people in this community had clearly been living in some kind of Eisenhower-era vacuum all their lives and didn't have even the vaguest concept of what real life was all about. They still celebrated Founders' Day here. They had a pumpkin festival coming up next month wherein they were holding a Sweetheart's Dance. That's actually what they were calling it—a Sweetheart's Dance.

Living in Endicott, he had quickly decided, was like being trapped forever in a Hayley Mills movie.

So, clearly, Angie Ellison couldn't possibly fully appreciate the precariousness of her situation. Which meant maybe Ethan ought to turn up the steam some.

"Angel," he began.

"'Angie,'" she corrected him quickly.

"Angel," he assured her with a confident nod. "We have a couple of ways we can go here."

She arched her brows in what he could only liken to curiosity, as if she were genuinely interested in hearing his suggestions. They might as well have been taking tea together, for all the concern she seemed to have for her imprisonment.

"Now, I know you didn't mistake my house for this Boomer whoever's place," he began again.

"Bumper," she interjected. "Bumper Shaugnessy."

"Whatever," he said wearily, feeling the gun in his hand begin to sag again. This time, he didn't bother to correct his aim. "I don't know why you're here, but I'm sure it has something to do with me."

She inclined her head forward. "And your name is…?" she asked.

He parted his lips slightly with his tongue and watched her thoughtfully. "Zorn," he finally told her. "Ethan Zorn."

She nodded, but seemed more fixed on what his mouth was doing than on what he was saying. He smiled. This was definitely getting interesting.

"It's very nice to meet you," she told him, sounding genuinely pleased to make his acquaintance. "Are you only visiting in Endicott? Do you have relatives here?"

"What I'm doing here, Angel—"

"'Angie.'"

"Angel, is really none of your business. However," he continued quickly when she opened her mouth to interrupt him again, "what *you're* doing in *my* house is very much my business. Especially since you keep avoiding the question."

"I'm not avoiding it," she told him. "I was just trying to make polite conversation."

"Thanks, but I'd rather make sense of this whole situation."

He edged closer to her on the bed, until his thigh was pressed against hers. Then he reached behind her to grab the bill of her cap, yanked it from her head and tossed it to the floor. A rich, rowdy stream of gold, copper and silver spilled down around her shoulders in loose spirals of curls, and she expelled a tiny, hiccuping sound of surprise. He smiled his most sinister smile as he reached for a handful of the soft, silky tresses at her nape, then wrapped them loosely in his fist.

He had no desire to get ugly. Angie Ellison seemed like a nice person, and he always did his best to refrain from roughing up nice people. Unfortunately, for the line of work he had chosen, roughing people up was near the top of requirements in his job description, and every now and then those people seemed perfectly nice. He hoped this wouldn't be one of those times.

"Now then," he said, trying once more, not quite able to ignore the softness of the hair he had wrapped around his fingers and the scent of spring flowers that had suddenly surrounded him the moment he'd freed the tangle of curls. "What are you doing in my house?"

The jig was up, Angie thought. Or whatever it was they said in those gangster films she used to sit through at the Roxy Theater on Willow Street when she was a teenager. Stalling wasn't working, and frankly, her brain was spinning from trying to make chitchat a viable source of survival. Ethan Zorn was starting to get impatient. And although she wasn't entirely sure what impatience did to mobsters, it was probably a safe bet to assume that it didn't much become them.

That assumption was reinforced when he bunched a fistful of her hair in his palm and tugged her head backward, then settled the muzzle of the gun against her throat.

"Tell me," he demanded.

"Oh," she gasped, her heartbeat hammering double time at the feel of the cool, hard metal nestled against her tender flesh.

This was *not* the way she had envisioned the evening turning out. When he tugged on her hair again, harder this time, Angie finally, finally began to understand exactly what she was up against. Not only had she gotten in way over her head, but she was about to be sucked down into a vast whirlpool of dark water unlike anything she'd ever encountered before.

"Please..." she petitioned softly, "you...you're hurting me."

To her complete mortification, tears sprang to her eyes—more a result of her fear than anything physically painful—and she bit her lip hard to prevent them from spilling. She did *not* want this man to see her cry. Crying was a sign of weakness, and she didn't want to appear weak to Ethan Zorn.

His hold on her hair loosened some at the sight of her tears, and his expression actually seemed to soften. Strange, she thought, that a gangster could look guilty and remorseful over something as simple as a woman's tears. But Ethan Zorn looked exactly that. After a moment, he removed the gun's muzzle from her neck, clicked on the safety and returned the weapon to its holster. But he continued to hold on to a handful of her hair, stroking a curl between thumb and forefinger, as if he'd discovered a magic talisman of some kind.

"Last chance," he told her, his voice low, but lacking in some of the menace it had carried earlier.

"All right," she ceded, finally understanding that there was no way he was going to let her go until she answered his questions. "Like I said, I'm Angie Ellison. And I...I work for the *Endicott Examiner.*"

"The newspaper?" he asked, seeming genuinely stunned by her revelation.

She nodded quickly. "I broke in here on purpose, knowing full well that this is your house."

He eyed her thoughtfully for a moment, then murmured, "Why?"

She swallowed hard and met his gaze, again surprised by the depth of the intelligence and emotion so evident there. Once again, he actually looked sorry to have manhandled her so, she marveled. He honestly seemed pained to have hurt her, however mildly.

"Because I know who you are," she told him.

He grinned, the crooked set to his mouth making him look oddly appealing. "And just who am I?"

Angie's heart began to beat more quickly. "You're Ethan Zorn. And you...you work for the mob."

His only reaction to her charge was a slight twitch to one cheek, and a vague darkening of his eyes. If she hadn't been as close to him as she was, she probably wouldn't have even noticed it. For a single, taut moment, he seemed frankly amazed by her assessment of him. Then, just as quickly, he became amused.

"The mob?" he repeated with a chuckle. "Is that what you think?"

"It's what I know."

"Angel, you have got one vivid imagination, I'll give you that."

"It's 'Angie,'" she corrected him irritably. Gun or no gun, she really hated being called "Angel," especially in the sexually charged, way-too-familiar manner in which Ethan Zorn said it. "And you do, too, work for the mob," she continued assuredly. "Don't bother to deny it, because I know you do."

He shook his head lightly. "I work for the Cokely Chemical Corporation," he told her. "I'm here on business for a few weeks. I'm a sales rep trying to drum up some new accounts."

"Riiiiight," she said, feeling a bit of her nerve return, now that he seemed to be relaxing some. "And Cokely always sends its sales reps out with big guns. I guess that's to guarantee winning over the potential client, isn't it?"

He glanced down at the gun, then back at Angie. "Traveling businessmen are easy targets," he told her. "I don't like to get caught off guard."

"Or maybe you just never know when you're going to have to off a snoopy journalist," she countered before she could stop herself.

"'Off a snoopy journalist'?" he echoed with a chuckle. "Angel, you've been watching too many Humphrey Bogart movies. I'm a sales rep for the Cokely Chemical Corporation. That's all there is to it."

"Oh, sure, that's your cover," she said with a nervous nod, wincing when she recalled, too late, that he continued to hold a fistful of her hair. "Look, my father owns a pharmaceutical manufacturing plant here, and you haven't called on him yet. Now, why would a sales rep overlook what would be his most lucrative client in town for more than two weeks? He wouldn't. My father's company would have been your first stop. It doesn't make sense. You don't work for Cokely."

"Okay, let's assume for a minute that I don't work for Cokely. Just how did you come to this conclusion that I work for the mob?"

"I have my sources."

"Yeah, well, obviously Cokely isn't one of them. If you'd

bothered to ask them, they would have told you I'm on their payroll and have been for years.''

''Yeah, they did tell me that, as a matter of fact.'' She paused for only a moment, then added, ''But like I said—I have other sources. And you could have just paid off someone in personnel to verify your employment, should someone ask about it.''

Ethan Zorn eyed her with much consideration, then freed the hair he had wound in his fist. Without speaking, he rose from the bed, strode carelessly to the desk on the other side of the room and retrieved a large white envelope from the blotter. Then he removed his wallet from his back pocket and flipped it open. He tossed that to the middle of the mattress, then lifted the envelope and spilled its entire contents beside it.

''My credentials,'' he said. ''Knock yourself out.''

Angie eyed him back warily, but she wasn't about to miss the opportunity to see what he had to offer. Gingerly, as she would a ticking bomb, she picked up his wallet and inspected his driver's license through the little plastic window that housed it. Pennsylvania. His address was a Philadelphia one that told her absolutely nothing, seeing as how she'd never been to Philadelphia before. But she memorized it quickly, knowing she could run a check on it tomorrow morning.

A number of credit cards—all of them gold—were tucked casually into each of the slots provided for such, and she inspected them one by one, noting that they were all stamped with the same name: Ethan Zorn. Feeling bolder, she started to peek into the money compartment, then lost her nerve and glanced up at him to silently ask permission first.

''Go ahead,'' he said. ''I told you. Knock yourself out.''

Oh, sure, she thought. That way, he wouldn't have to do it himself.

She tucked her thumb into the money section, fingering each of the neatly lined-up bills as she added them, noting vaguely that they were all in order of descending amount, and that each of the presidents was right side up and facing forward.

An anal-retentive mobster, she thought mildly. Now, that was a good one.

Three hundred seventy-eight dollars, she tallied, and, presumably, change. Now, what kind of person walked around with that kind of money in cash? Immediately, she answered herself: mobsters, that's what kind. She glanced up at him again and saw that he was smiling.

"I don't like to use traveler's checks," he said, clearly understanding her unasked question.

"Why not? Because they can be traced?"

"Credit cards can be traced, too," he stated, nodding toward his collection.

"Yeah, if you use them," she said. "Who says these aren't just for show?"

He shook his head, clearly thinking she was an idiot. Angie frowned.

"Let's just say I don't like having my name bandied about," he told her.

"A private person, are you?"

"Yeah, you could say that."

"I suppose I could, but I bet you don't use traveler's checks—or credit cards—for another reason entirely."

He sighed. "And that reason would be?"

"Because you're connected."

He laughed, a dry, eerie sound that was in no way convincing. "And what would a mobster like me be doing in a place like this?"

She met his gaze with what she hoped was steely-eyed determination. "To get your dirty hands on my father's pharmaceutical company."

His smile was smug and indulgent, the kind a resigned mother might offer a two-year-old who was turning blue from holding his breath for the hundredth time. "I see. And why would I want my hands on your father's pharmaceutical company?"

"So you—and the mob—can use it to further your filthy drug trade."

This time his laughter was an out-and-out bark of disbelief. "You have *got* to be kidding."

"Don't bother to deny it," Angie told him, irritated at his light mood. "I know that's why you're here."

"Angel, I'm here trying to expand Cokely's business, that's all. This town is perfectly situated for me to hit a lot of small communities in three states in one trip." After a moment's pause, he added, "You say your father owns a pharmaceutical company? Could you give him my card?"

"Very funny."

"Hey, I'm serious. I need all the help I can get here. And for all you know, Cokely could give him a much better deal than his current chemical supplier."

"Thanks anyway, but my father doesn't deal with criminals."

Ethan Zorn shook his head and pointed toward the pile of information scattered on his bed. "Will you just have a look at all that? I'm exactly who I say I am. Trust me."

Oh, sure, Angie thought. The last guy who had asked her to trust him had had her flat on her back in the front seat of his car in about thirty seconds. Fortunately for her, that self-defense course had paid off, and she'd planted her knee in his groin with fairly little effort. Something told her, however, that Ethan Zorn was more than prepared for such a maneuver, should she try it on him.

Nevertheless, she gazed down at the multicolored, variously sized scraps of paper and plastic that dotted the bedspread. A corporate ID from Cokely that looked to be authentic, various work orders, maps of Endicott and its surrounding communities, invitations to call on local businesses and representatives from the chamber of commerce, even a letter from the mayor oozing with compliments and boasts of how business friendly the little town of Endicott, Indiana, could be.

Okay, so a lot of this stuff made Ethan Zorn seem that he was nothing more than a sales rep for the Cokely Chemical Corporation. Angie was still suspicious. As she'd told him a moment ago, she had her sources. And she'd done some sleuthing of her own. And she had good reason to believe he was, in reality, exactly who she'd accused him of being.

"Satisfied?" he asked when she looked up at him again.

She began to slide all his credentials back into the envelope from which they had spilled, and avoided meeting his eyes. "No," she told him simply. "It's not difficult to forge these things."

"You think I'd forge a letter from your mayor?"

She shrugged. "Maybe."

"Then why don't you give her a call and ask her if she's been in contact with me about local business?"

"Maybe I will."

"Ms. Ellison—" he began.

When he stopped abruptly and said nothing else, Angie halted her own activities and looked up at him. His expression changed drastically then, and this time he was the one to smack his forehead soundly with his palm. She hoped her own earlier effort had been a bit more convincing than his was.

"Wait a minute," he said with a laugh. "Sure. Now I know. You say your last name is Ellison?"

She nodded tightly.

"Ellison Pharmaceuticals," he stated knowledgeably. "I'm calling on them Friday."

"You've been in Endicott for more than two weeks, and you're just now getting around to calling on my father?" she asked, reiterating her earlier doubt.

Her question seemed to stump him for a moment, but he covered admirably. "I've had a lot of preliminary legwork to do. Plus, I had to go back to Philadelphia briefly. Just got back tonight, in fact."

"Uh-huh."

Instead of responding to her murmur of doubt, he extended a hand harmlessly toward her, as if he were doing nothing more than reaching forward to help her out of a car. And Angie took a good look at him for the first time since being discovered in his room—a *good* look.

His shirt hung open over a broad chest, liberally dusted with dark hair that disappeared below the waistband of his trousers. His legs were long, and despite the baggy trousers, she knew somehow that they'd be spectacularly formed. The forearms visible beneath the rolled-up sleeves of his shirt were truly works of art, ridges of muscle corded with strong veins. And his hands... Angie bit back a sigh. Who would have suspected a killer could have such incredibly sexy hands?

An odd heat wound through her as she processed the information she'd collected about his physique, and she suddenly became aware of him as a man instead of a threat. Since he'd come to Endicott, she'd viewed him only from a distance. Now, up close and personal at last, she realized that she was out of her league in more ways than one.

He had the face of an angel, she decided as her gaze lingered there. A fallen angel, granted, but an angel nonetheless. His wasn't the kind of face she associated with the mob. His eyes were dark and dreamy and beautiful, his nose straight and narrow and obviously never broken in a fistfight—something she might have expected of a man like him. His mouth was full and utterly masculine, bracketed by deep slashes she normally only associated with movie stars. His lashes were thick and even blacker than his hair somehow, his jaw lean and cleanly defined.

All in all, with his expensive Italian clothes so casually thrown askew and his heavy-lidded, deeply sultry gaze, he looked like an ad for Versace in *GQ*. There was no way—no way—anyone would ever convince her that this man was a sales rep. With all due respect to sales reps everywhere, this guy was just too...too...too...

Too.

That's all there was to it. But somehow, now that she'd actually interacted with him on a personal level, he didn't seem like a mobster, either. What exactly he *was*, she honestly didn't know, but... Could she possibly be mistaken about him? she wondered. Could there be any way her sources were wrong?

He was still standing before her, silently reaching out to

her, and without even thinking about what she was doing, Angie lifted her hand to place it in his. Immediately, he folded his fingers over hers, and her pale, delicate hand was completely swallowed by his dark, rawboned one. His skin was warm and rough, his grip confident and possessive. And it occurred to Angie then that if he ever set his mind to it, he could do or be whatever he wanted in this world.

"Thanks," she muttered absently as he gave her a gentle tug.

He hauled her easily off the bed, but when she would have halted her progress on the spot where her feet first hit the floor, Ethan Zorn continued to pull her forward, propelling her against his chest.

"Oops," he said blandly, catching her capably in his arms.

He folded them over her back with much familiarity, and tilted his head down toward hers with what she could only liken to intent. Intent to do what, she hesitated to consider, but intent nonetheless.

"Do you mind?" she muttered as she tried to squirm out of his embrace.

"Not at all," he assured her, tightening his hold.

She doubled up her fists against his bare chest, trying not to notice the warm vitality and rigid definition of the numerous and well-formed muscles she encountered. Trying, and failing miserably.

"That's not what I meant," she said as she began to push herself away again.

But he continued to hold her easily in place, even managed somehow to pull her a bit closer. "Hey, you're the one who climbed into my bed," he noted. "I'm just moving things along to their logical conclusion. Shouldn't I assume you're as interested in something like this as I am? You yourself said you've been admiring me from afar. And you know, it gets pretty lonely sometimes when you're a traveling sales rep."

She ceased her struggles for a moment and tipped her head back to glare at him. "You should assume nothing," she told him. "I have *not* been admiring you from afar, and I don't care how lonely you get."

"But you said you've been admiring me from—"

"I lied, okay? Big surprise, right? You admitted yourself you didn't believe me when I said it."

He dipped his head lower toward hers and murmured, "I think I've decided now that I will believe you after all. You just don't seem like the dishonest type."

Angie ignored that, countering instead, "And I did *not* climb *in*to your bed."

He cocked one eyebrow in a silent request for clarification, and seeing as how he had sort of found her where he had, Angie supposed she owed him at least some small explanation.

"I climbed *on*to your bed," she told him. "*Big* difference."

"Not to my way of thinking." He tightened his hold on her even more and tilted his head ever so slightly to one side, as if he fully intended to kiss her. "You sure you don't want me to tie you up?" he asked, his voice low and level and completely serious.

Angie's heart began to beat faster, rushing blood to warm parts of her body that in no way needed warming. His breath fanned her forehead, and his muscular arms were draped around her shoulders and down her back with a familiarity suggesting that was precisely where they belonged. His fingers skimmed against her fanny in a way that *might* have been casual, but then again, might not have been. And all she could do was stand there letting him get away with it, wondering what it would be like to be very casual indeed with the man.

God help her, she was actually turned on by him, she realized with no small amount of shock. Utterly, irrevocably, turned on. By a mobster. She was responding with a needful, almost visceral desire to mate with a man who—although incredibly good-looking, sexy even, in a strange, he-man kind of way that most self-respecting women would *never* admit to finding attractive—would just as soon shoot her as make love to her.

She had to start getting out more—that was all there was to it.

"No," she assured him, only half remembering what it was she was objecting to. Boy, his eyes were amazing.

"No, you don't want me to tie you up?" he asked softly. "Or no, you're not sure? Because if you're not sure, Angel, then maybe we should—"

"No, I don't want you to tie me up," she quickly cut him off, the assurance sounding less than convincing, even to her own ears. "And it's *Angie,* not Angel."

He smiled, but made no other concession to her correction. "Well, like I said. Maybe some other time."

But he still didn't release her. And for one long, lingering moment, Angie didn't even try to struggle or insist that he let her go. In fact, for one long, lingering moment, all she did was stand there letting him hold her, wishing way back in the very back of her brain that he really was a sales rep for the Cokely Chemical Corporation, and that she was head of the Endicott Chamber of Commerce.

Then she could do something with him right now that some dark, delirious part of her really wanted to do, and she could tell herself it was only for the good of the community, something that would create jobs and boost the local economy, something that was in fact her civic duty.

And that was when it occurred to her that there really must be something to that one myth about Bob. Naturally, she'd witnessed for herself that the comet made people say and do things they'd never do under usual circumstances. But now, as ridiculous as it seemed, she was beginning to believe that other myth, too, and thinking that maybe Bob really did create love relationships between people who would normally never be attracted to each other.

Damned comet.

While Angie was still pondering that, Ethan Zorn dipped his head lower to rest his forehead against hers. "You know," he murmured, his voice a quiet caress, "I oughta call the cops and have you arrested for breaking into my house."

Helplessly, Angie slanted her own head so that her mouth lay only inches away from his. "But you won't," she said with a soft sigh, "because you're connected to the mob, and you don't want to have any more to do with the cops than you have to. Even the local boys."

He shook his head slowly, a gesture that brought his lips even closer to hers. "No," he whispered, "I won't call them because it's just not worth my time."

"Oh, sure, that's *your* excuse."

"For that, maybe," he said. "But I have no excuse for this."

And before Angie could object—not that she necessarily wanted to, anyway—Ethan Zorn kissed her. Just lowered his head to close up those last few millimeters that separated them, and covered her mouth with his.

She responded instinctively and without thinking, tipping her head back to afford him better access, lifting a hand to thread her fingers easily through his hair. For a single, thoughtless instant, she succumbed to her feelings instead of her reason, and in that single, thoughtless instant, she got the ride of her life.

A hazy, liquid warmth filled her, traveling to every extreme in her body, bubbling through her veins to effervesce in her heart like a natural spring of emotion. His lips barely grazed hers, a soft brush of heat against heat, over and over and over, but Angie felt the repercussions of his caress to the very depth of her soul. And all she could do was marvel that such a man could be so utterly gentle, so tentative and tender.

And then she ceased to wonder at all, because she wanted to focus instead on the feel of him surrounding her.

Ethan was too busy enjoying himself to wonder much about anything, especially about what had come over him to kiss Angie the Angel the way he had. Although some vague part of him knew that what he was doing was the height of stupidity, he simply couldn't quite bring himself to put an end to it just yet. She responded to him in a way that no other woman had before, opening to him completely, fully trusting him to do the right thing.

Bastard, he berated himself. You should be ashamed of yourself, taking advantage of a nice girl like her.

But his conscience was in no way chastised. It simply reminded him that Angie the Angel had been in his bed, after all, and she wasn't exactly shoving him away and shouting, "Masher!" now, was she?

Nevertheless, he forced himself to end the kiss before they could carry it too far, then made himself take a step away from her. He watched as she blinked a few times, then seemed to adjust her focus back to the task at hand. He had expected her to be outraged by what he had done. Instead, she seemed to be disappointed that he had stopped. But she said nothing to confirm either reaction.

"Yeah, maybe next time," he said softly, "we can try that tying-up business. For now, though..." He paused meaningfully, took a step forward again to bring his body up flush with hers and lifted his hand to trace her lower lip with his thumb. "For now, maybe we should just get to know each other a little better."

Angie Ellison only stared at him in complete bemusement for a moment, then he thought she nodded just the tiniest bit.

"I need to get going," she finally said, as if the two of them had just been out on a date, and she hadn't, in fact, been breaking and entering and accusing him of being a mobster looking to further his drug trade.

Ethan nodded. "I'll call you."

She nodded back. "Okay."

And then she crossed the room in total silence, to where he had tossed the door key earlier. But instead of picking it up to unlock the door and let herself out, she hoisted herself up onto the window ledge and straddled it. Briefly, she looked over at Ethan, and he would have sold his soul—what little he hadn't bargained away already—to know what she was thinking. If she was even half as foggy-headed and befuddled as he was right now, it probably wasn't a good idea for her to be dangling from a second-story window.

But before he could stop her, and with an expertise that surprised him, she twisted and dropped from the window. For a moment, all he could see were two sets of black-gloved fingers gripping the windowsill. Then one of those disappeared, followed by the other, and he was left alone in the room to wonder if he hadn't just dreamed the entire episode.

He'd only half listened to the rumblings in town about the comet whose regular fifteen-year return Endicott was now celebrating. He'd heard ol' Bob was responsible for a number of odd developments, not the least of which was making people do the most unusual, extraordinary things, things they would *never,* not in a million years, do otherwise. At the time, however, he'd thought the locals were just feeding him a line, hoping he'd buy into the myth, and therefore the celebration, and spend a lot of his tourist dollars to hang around for the comet's climax.

Now he was beginning to wonder if maybe there wasn't something to all the comet mumbo-jumbo after all.

Because try as he might, he sure as hell couldn't think of a single reason for why he had done what he'd just done. Why he had kissed Angie Ellison, nosy journalist, daughter of the man he was there to check out, all-around decent woman and upstanding citizen. It was almost as if in kissing her, he had been trying to save himself from eternal perdition. If his superiors ever got wind of this, they'd kill him.

But of all the crazy ideas speeding pell-mell through Ethan's head at the moment, one thought alone kept circling above the others with alarming regularity.

How could she possibly have known that he was here at the behest of the mob, and that he had come to Endicott to scope out her father's pharmaceutical company and its potential to further their drug trade?

Three

Angie woke up the next morning with the oddest sense of well-being. Her pillow and mattress felt softer than they ever had before, and her cotton sheets seemed to have somehow turned to silk. A subtle breeze, redolent of freshly mown lawn and the onset of autumn, nudged aside the curtains of the open window above her head, and a purple finch sang happily nearby. Even at such an early hour, children were laughing in the playground of the school across the street, and she could hear the sound of jazz music tumbling from the window of a neighboring apartment.

What an absolutely delicious way to wake up, she thought as she stretched her arms above her head and flexed every muscle from shoulder to toe. And what a supremely glorious day. The sun was shining, the air was warm and welcoming, children were laughing, the birds were singing and—

—and she'd kissed a mobster last night.

The realization exploded in Angie's brain with the force of an atomic bomb. She froze in midstretch, snapped her eyes

wide open and gazed panic-stricken at the ceiling overhead.
With agonizing clarity, she replayed in her head every tem-
pestuous moment following her discovery by Ethan Zorn, cul-
minating in that single, delirious kiss just before she let herself
out through the bedroom window.

Oh, God, had she actually done that? she thought frantically
as she squeezed her eyes shut once again and tried fruitlessly
to bury herself in the mattress. Had she actually let him kiss
her? Had she actually kissed him back? And, oh, no, had she
actually insinuated that she wanted him to tie her up?

Angie expelled a long, heartfelt groan and covered her eyes
with loose fists. She'd ruined everything. In addition to making a complete fool of herself, Ethan Zorn was onto her now,
and he was going to be watching his back. Any opportunity
she'd had to catch him off guard, to trip him up and expose
him for the low-life, scumbag, murdering slug that he was,
she'd blown.

He was trying to take her father's company, she reminded
herself. Confiscate it for the mob. For all she knew, part of
his plan was to put her father—her entire family, even—on
ice to get his grubby paws on Ellison Pharmaceuticals.

And she'd *kissed* him, she recalled yet again. She'd pressed
her lips hungrily against those of a man who was probably
more familiar with kisses of death than kisses of passion. Ick.
Worse than that, she hardly knew him. What on earth must he
think of her?

Ethan Zorn was a *criminal,* for God's sake, she reminded
herself. And she was worrying about what he was going to
think of *her* morals? Nevertheless, she found herself honestly
concerned that he probably considered her to be a simple-
minded, sex-starved journalistic dilettante. After all, she certainly felt like one at the moment.

"I am *not* a dilettante," she asserted out loud. She dropped
her hands from her eyes and jackknifed up in bed, deciding
not to evaluate her other dubious self-professed traits at the
moment. "I am a serious journalist who's hot on the trail of
a story that's going to blow the lid off this town."

If Ethan Zorn didn't blow her lid first.

She groaned again. Not just at the knowledge of what she'd done the night before. But at the realization that she'd enjoyed it *so much.* That damned comet, she tried to console herself. It was all Bob's fault. Under normal circumstances, she'd never look twice at a man like Ethan Zorn. Bob always messed with the citizens of Endicott when he came around.

If she tried hard, she could almost make herself believe that Bob was the reason she'd succumbed to a criminal the night before. Unfortunately, a not-so-little part of her was still too busy being preoccupied by what it had felt like to be wrapped in the cocoon that was Ethan Zorn. She recalled the strength in the arms that had pulled her close, remembered the soft brush of his lips as his mouth claimed hers, replayed every erratic thump of her heart and the way it had rushed heat to every body part.

She groaned a third time. How could such an evil man have made her feel so *good?*

"Just don't think about it, Angie," she instructed herself.

Then she responded to herself immediately, Oh, sure. That ought to be no problem at all. Kiss a felon, embrace a guy with blood on his hands and probably in the trunk of his car, and just forget all about it. Yeah, right. Uh-huh. Okeydokey. Whatever.

She shoved herself out of bed and quickly showered and dressed for work, opting to look halfway professional today in a pair of baggy beige trousers and a sleeveless coral pink blouse. As an afterthought, she yanked an ivory blazer from the closet, just in case it cooled off some. September in southern Indiana was iffy. And living right on the river, it was impossible for anyone to tell what the weather would bring from one day to the next.

As she passed through the kitchen, she snagged a box of Pop-Tarts from the cupboard and shook a couple free to have for breakfast. She was still clutching half of the second one between her teeth when she exited her front door, making sure to lock it behind herself, because you just never knew about some people. Then she turned toward the elevators across the hall and halted in her tracks.

Ethan Zorn was standing there waiting for her.

The pastry in her mouth turned to paste, and although she swallowed, she felt it lodge halfway down her esophagus. She swallowed again—several times, in fact—and after some difficulty, she finally managed to free the clump of dough. Then, as unobtrusively as she could—which really wasn't very unobtrusive at all—she quickly tucked the rest of the Pop-Tart into the pocket of her trousers.

Although instinct told her to retreat immediately back into her apartment and barricade herself inside with what meager living-room furniture she owned, Angie stood firm before her front door and tried not to panic. But Ethan Zorn just stared at her from ten feet away, his posture insouciant, his expression inscrutable.

He was leaning back against the wall beside the elevator, his feet crossed at his ankles, his hands shoved deep into the pockets of his charcoal tailored trousers. His suit jacket hung open over a stark white dress shirt and a silk necktie patterned with geometric shapes in muted blues, burgundies and greens. He had shaven, she noted, and an odd pang of disappointment opened up inside her at the realization. He'd looked so adorably rough, so wonderfully imperfect, with a shadow of a beard darkening his face last night. Clean-shaven as he was now, he was almost too handsome.

Almost.

But there was still too much of the troublemaker, the seducer, the criminal element, dancing in his dark eyes. He was laughing at her. Somehow Angie was certain that she was the butt of some private joke that he was enjoying immensely, and the knowledge of that made her frown.

Sales rep my eye, she thought, ogling his jacket and trousers again. She had worked her way through college selling men's clothing at Buddy's Man About Town shop, so she knew her men's ready-to-wear better than she knew her own. Ethan Zorn must receive some pretty primo commissions if he could attire himself in twelve-hundred-dollar suits and hundred-dollar neckties. She'd seen the little red job he was driving around town, too. And she couldn't recall any corporation on the planet that handed out Porsches for company cars.

"What are you doing here?" she demanded, polite behavior the last thing on her mind at the moment. "How did you find out where I live?"

He pushed himself away from the wall and sauntered leisurely toward her. "A handy little item I found on top of my refrigerator. The phone book. Maybe you've heard of it?"

She narrowed her eyes at him. Okay, so she'd set herself up for that one. "Are you following me?" she asked.

He smiled. "Not yet. You haven't gone anywhere."

She rolled her eyes heavenward. "Are you *planning* on following me?"

He lifted his shoulders and dropped them again. "Depends on where you plan to go."

"I'm going to work," she said.

"Need a lift?"

She shook her head. "Nope."

"How about dinner later?"

"No, I won't need a lift there, either."

He dipped his head forward to acknowledge her dodge. "Actually, I meant how about having dinner with me later?"

"Can't," she said, hoping she sounded breezy and uninterested in spite of the way her heart was hip-hopping around in her chest like mad.

"Why not?" he wanted to know.

She smiled back, smugly, she hoped. "I already have a date for dinner."

He leaned forward a bit, his gaze pinning her to the spot. "Cancel it."

She arched her eyebrows in surprise at his forwardness. "Excuse me?"

He withdrew his hands from his pockets, propped one on his hip and planted the other ever so casually against the wall beside her head. Then he leaned toward her even more, way too close for comfort, not to mention propriety. "Cancel it," he repeated softly.

She gaped at his audacity and took a step backward to give herself some room. Unfortunately, her action simply resulted in her backing right into her front door and banging the back of her head against it. Hard. She winced.

"Boy, you are some piece of work, you know that?" she asked as she gingerly rubbed the injured spot on her scalp.

He smiled again and took a step forward, invading her space even more. "So I've been told. What time should I pick you up after work?"

She shook her head slowly. "I am *not* having dinner with you. Later or ever. I don't eat out with criminals."

"Fine," he said. "We'll eat in. Not many people know this, but I'm a terrific cook. How about my place, tonight at, oh…say…sevenish?"

Sevenish? she echoed to herself. What kind of self-respecting mobster used such a word? She made a mental note to call her friend Maury—her source—as soon as she got to work. Maybe Ethan Zorn was exactly who he claimed to be. Maybe he really was nothing more than a sales rep for Cokely. In which case, she thought further, taking in the way his broad chest strained at the buttons of his shirt, and the shadow of rough hair beneath, dinner didn't seem like such a bad idea after all.

Stop it, she instructed herself. *He's exactly who you think he is, and you'd better be on your guard.* At least, she *probably* ought to be on her guard, she thought. Possibly. Maybe.

He said nothing more after extending his invitation, just continued to loom over Angie, staring at her mouth as if he had some long-term plans for it. She really wished he'd stop looking at her like that. Not just because it made her stomach do all kinds of funny flip-flops, but because it gave her all kinds of ideas she really shouldn't be having, regardless of who he was.

"Why did you come here?" she asked him again, marveling that her voice actually sounded almost normal.

He drew in a deep breath and released it slowly, letting his gaze rove easily over her face. "I wanted to make sure you were okay," he finally said softly. "That you made it home safe and sound last night." He hesitated for only a moment before adding, "A woman living alone can't be too careful these days."

She narrowed her eyes at him. "Is that a threat?"

He shook his head. "No, Angel, that's a fact of life."

Her stomach caught fire at the way he uttered the nickname he had chosen for her. "Don't call me that," she told him, her voice lacking all conviction.

"Why not? Because you're no angel?"

She swallowed again, the pasty pastry in her stomach now turning to cement. "I'm as clean-cut as they come," she assured him.

He chuckled at that, a low, languid sound that rumbled up from a deep, dark place inside him. "Now, *that* I believe," he said. The hand he had settled on his hip rose slowly toward her face, and he skimmed his fingertips over her lower lip. "And it really is too bad," he added softly.

The gentle caress of his fingertips was almost more than Angie could bear. Her eyes fluttered closed for a moment, and she allowed herself the guilty pleasure of enjoying his warm touch for just a brief instant. Then slowly, reluctantly, she turned her head to the side and opened her eyes again. But his touch followed her, his index finger lingering at the fullest curve of her lip.

"Too bad for you?" she asked, more than a little breathless. "Or for me?"

He eyed her thoughtfully for a moment, then told her, "Maybe it's too bad for both of us."

She jerked her head backward to escape the subtle seduction of his fingers...and banged her head on her front door again.

"Ow," she muttered, lifting her hand to her scalp again. She frowned at Ethan. "Will you please just go away and leave me alone?"

Once more, his smile returned, warming parts of her that

had no business feeling warm. "I'll go away," he said, taking a step away from her. "For now, at least. But I don't think I'm going to be able to leave you alone."

Angie really wanted to say something in response to that. Truly she did. But she couldn't think of a single witty retort. Or even a boring retort, for that matter. All she could do was stand there in bemused silence and watch as Ethan Zorn turned and walked toward the stairwell, ignoring the elevator behind him.

And all she could think was, *Thank goodness you won't be leaving me alone. I was afraid I was going to have to go through all this comet weirdness by myself.*

Rosemary was already sitting at their usual table in the back of the Maple Leaf Café when Angie entered it that evening. She didn't see Kirby, however, so assumed her other friend must be running even later than she was herself. Which was just as well. It would be easier to steer the conversation toward some vague, meaningless topic with only one other person to worry about. By the time Kirby showed up, with any luck at all, the name Ethan Zorn wouldn't have cropped up anywhere in the conversation.

Rosemary greeted her absently as she sat down, and a waitress appeared immediately to take Angie's drink order. She asked for her usual, and automatically withdrew five sugar packets from the bowl on the table, giving them a vigorous shake in preparation for the waitress's return. Except that when the waitress returned, she wasn't carrying Angie's usual.

She grabbed the server's arm before the other woman could get away. "Stephanie," she said as she eyed the murky, brownish liquid cautiously. "What *is* this…stuff…you brought me?"

Stephanie shrugged. "It's your usual. Prune juice and lemonade with a splash of Angostura and a shot of Jack Daniel's."

Angie tried not to gag. "That is *not* my usual."

Stephanie smacked her forehead hard with the heel of her

free hand. "You're right. Prune juice and lemonade with a splash of Angostura and a shot of Jack Daniel's is Tippy Brody's usual." She reached for Angie's glass. "Boy, I'll tell ya—that Bob has just been messing with my head for a week now. I can't seem to keep any of my orders straight."

"Tell me about it," Angie concurred. "I broke into some-one's house last night, myself."

"That Bob," Stephanie said, punctuating the observation with a laugh and a negligent swipe of her hand. "He is *such* a kidder."

"Don't I know it."

The waitress sighed. "I must have given Tippy your iced tea. I'll bring you a fresh one."

"Thanks."

Once Angie had her iced tea and had fixed it the way she liked it, she turned to Rosemary with a playful grin. "Hey, I heard through the grapevine at the newspaper that your old lab partner and favorite nemesis, Willis Random, is back in town."

Rosemary glanced up, her chin-length, dark brown curls bobbing with the action, and she narrowed her eyes angrily at her friend. "Oh, yeah, he's back. That twerp. He's an astro-physicist now with five damned degrees, which, of course, is absolutely no surprise. He's here to study Bob." After a mo-ment, she added, "And to make my life miserable."

"How does he look?" Angie asked. "Is he still a pizza face?"

Rosemary's expression changed, to something Angie couldn't quite interpret. "Not hardly," she spat venomously.

When her friend didn't elaborate and instead yanked a roll from the breadbasket and began to tear at it with a bit more force than was necessary to break it in two, Angie asked fur-ther, "So?"

Rosemary studied her dinner roll intently, then lifted her knife to butter it. Except that when she went to spread the froth of pale yellow across the bread, she accidentally—at least, Angie assumed it was an accident—drove the knife deep into its middle.

"So what?" Rosemary snapped.

"So, spill, Rosemary. What's the poop with Willis?"

The other woman continued to impale her dinner roll as she hissed, "Oh, what, you mean besides the fact that he saw me in my underwear?"

Angie gaped at her friend. "Willis Random saw you in your underwear? How did that happen?"

Rosemary stabbed her roll again. "I don't want to talk about it."

Angie was about to press the issue further, when Kirby approached the table with a rather brisk, irregular stride. Shafts of straight, pale-blond hair danced around her shoulders as she glanced worriedly behind herself, as if the hounds of hell were nipping at her heels. She, too, had a funny look on her face, and Angie wasn't quite sure what to make of it, either.

"Hey, Kirb," she greeted her other friend. "What's new?"

Kirby dropped into her chair and snatched up her menu, her gaze ricocheting from one face to the other before dropping back to her menu. "Nothing," she said coolly. "Sorry I'm late."

Angie glanced over at Rosemary curiously, but the other woman only shrugged to indicate she didn't understand Kirby's behavior, either.

After a moment of somewhat stilted silence, Rosemary piped up, "Now that you're both here, I have some good gossip. Want to hear?"

Both Angie and Kirby grumbled something in the affirmative.

Rosemary's expression was mischievous as she reported, "Being a travel agent has *finally* netted me something interesting. Guess who I booked rooms for here in town? Guess who's come to Endicott for the comet festival? You'll never guess."

"Who?" Angie asked.

"You'll never guess," Rosemary told her.

"Give me a hint."

"He's an international celebrity," Rosemary revealed. "A rowdy playboy with a baaaaaad reputation. He's rich, he's famous, he's gorgeous, he's eccentric, he's a comet buff and amateur astronomer... Oh, you'll never guess. Not in a million billion—"

"James Nash."

Rosemary gaped at Kirby, and Angie grew even more confused.

"How did *you* know James is in town?" Rosemary demanded.

"He's in town," was all Kirby said in response.

"You've seen him?" Angie asked. "You've seen James Nash? In the flesh?" For some, it was the equivalent of an Elvis sighting.

"I've not only seen him, I've met him," Kirby affirmed, still looking at her menu instead of at her friends.

"You've *met* him?" Angie and Rosemary said as one.

Kirby only nodded once.

"So?" Angie asked.

"So what?"

Angie expelled an impatient sound. "So give us the gory details," she said.

Kirby glared at her, then bit out through gritted teeth, "He saw me naked, okay? Is that gory enough for you?"

The other women only stared at her for a moment, openmouthed and dumbfounded. Finally, Rosemary managed to say, "James Nash saw you naked? But, Kirby, *no* man in Endicott has seen you naked." After a moment, she added as a qualifier, "I mean, not that you haven't *tried....*"

"James Nash has, all right?" Kirby growled.

"How on earth did that happen?" Angie demanded.

Kirby returned her attention to her menu. "I don't want to talk about it."

Angie made a face. "What is it with you two today? I spilled my guts about Ethan Zorn and told you all about his mob connections when he first crawled out from under his rock. Now I wanna hear about your guys. I think I'm entitled to that.''

Kirby looked at Rosemary, who was suddenly *very* preoccupied with her own menu. ''Rosemary has a guy?'' she asked. ''Who?''

''Willis Random is back in town,'' Angie said with a knowing grin.

''You're kidding,'' Kirby replied with a chuckle. ''Is he still a pizza-faced little twerp?''

''I don't know,'' Angie told her. ''Ask Rosemary.''

Kirby turned to her other friend. ''Is Willis still a pizza-faced little twerp?''

''I don't want to talk about it,'' Rosemary said. Instead she turned the tables. ''What's James Nash like?''

Kirby lifted her chin defiantly. ''I don't want to talk about it.''

Both women glanced back down at their menus, and Angie stared at them both. ''But—'' she began.

''I don't want to talk about it,'' the two women chorused.

Then Rosemary looked up again. ''How about you?''

Angie stiffened in her chair. ''What about me?'' she asked, feigning confusion.

''How did your midnight express into Ethan Zorn's house go last night?''

This time Angie was the one to pick up her menu and study it. ''I don't want to talk about it,'' she said.

''But, Angie—''

Angie kept her gaze trained on her menu and ignored her friend's interjection. ''So what's the special today?''

Ethan Zorn returned to his house that night with visions of Angie the Angel still dancing in his head. Unfortunately, each and every one of them was dashed away when he saw the phone messages fanned out on his desk to greet him.

Mrs. Mack's aged handwriting wasn't the best in the world, but there were only two people who could be calling him at this number. And the way things had been going for him lately, he could pretty well guess which one these notes were from, even without the unmistakable *P* that began the name on each one.

Dammit. He had been hoping the big boys wouldn't hear about last night's episode with Angie until later. He should have known better. Those guys knew everything.

He picked up the phone and dialed a long string of numbers, then worked to loosen his necktie as he awaited a response from the other end of the line. And while the steady burr of the ringing resounded in his ear, his mind began to wander inevitably back to thoughts of an angel.

As a result, he became more than a little preoccupied, and was caught somewhat off guard by the gruffly offered "Palmieri here" when it came over the other end of the line.

Ethan straightened quickly, even though a good seven hundred miles separated him from his superior. "Zorn checking in," he replied, hoping his voice carried none of the disdain he felt whenever he had to speak to Denny Palmieri.

"Get rid of the Ellison woman," Palmieri told him without preamble. "I don't know how she found out about our little operation, and frankly, I don't care. Just get rid of her. Whatever you have to do, do it. I want her out of the picture. Now."

Ethan shook his head. How the hell did they find out about stuff like this so quickly? he wondered. Either they had the house bugged, something he'd been checking for daily, or else they were outside in a van somewhere with a high-powered microphone. It was driving him nuts trying to stay one step ahead of them.

"She's harmless," he said into the phone, hoping he was telling the truth. Angie Ellison was small-time to be sure. But he got the impression that she was also as tenacious as a pit bull when it came to getting what she wanted.

"She's onto us," his boss countered. "Obviously we underestimated the locals. We can't have her poking around. It'll ruin everything."

"She doesn't know anything," Ethan assured the other man. "She's seen *The Godfather* too many times, and she has a vivid imagination. Add that to growing up in a place like this, where nothing exciting ever happens, and you get yourself a woman who has wild ideas. Period.''

"She's been nosing around like Pavlov's dog," Palmieri said.

Instead of pointing out to his superior that Pavlov's dog and nosing around had absolutely nothing to do with each other, Ethan simply reiterated, "She's no threat to us. Trust me."

"How can you be so sure?"

"I've met her."

"And?"

Ethan chuckled, a heartfelt sound. "She's cute, Denny. Cute. Nothing to worry about."

"I got a bad feeling about her."

Ethan had feelings about her, too, he realized. And none of them was particularly good, either. "Look, I can handle Angel Ellison."

"I thought her name was Angie."

"Right," he corrected himself immediately, kicking himself for the stupid slip. "Angie. I can handle her."

"You sure?"

"I'm sure."

"I don't like this, Ethan. Not one bit."

"Will you please just let me take care of things at this end and stop worrying?"

"This is the first time we've turned you loose to act as your own man," his boss reminded him. "You still haven't proved yourself flying solo. Don't screw up."

"Have I ever let you down in the past?"

Clearly with some reluctance, Palmieri sighed and answered, "No."

"And I'm not gonna start now," Ethan assured him. "Angie Ellison is an amateur in this game. She's a novice. She's meaningless. She's nothing." He swallowed hard after uttering the lie and hoped he wasn't laying it on too thick. Angie's safety could be at stake here. "Forget about her," he told the other man.

His assurance was met by a lengthy pause from the other end of the line. Then, "I still think we should just do the easy thing and get rid of her."

Ethan bit down hard to stop himself from overreacting. "This is a peaceful, sleepy little town, Denny. And Angie Ellison is known and loved by all. If she disappears, it's gonna draw a public outcry, and we're gonna wind up drawing attention we can't afford to have. I can handle her," he repeated emphatically.

Another hesitation from his boss, then, "You'd better, Zorn. Or I'll see to it that both of you are taken care of."

Big talk, Ethan told himself. That's all Palmieri ever did was talk. He left the dirty work to his underlings. Like Ethan. Still, the reminder brought him little comfort.

"I'll be seeing her father tomorrow," he told his boss. "I'll have more for you after that."

"Yeah, you do that," Palmieri said. "I want a full report of your progress. And Ethan," he added, his voice low and menacing now.

"Yeah?"

"Keep a close eye on the girl."

He was unable to help the smile that curled his lips when he considered how much he was going to enjoy that part of the assignment, at least. "Oh, you can count on me doing just that," he told Palmieri. "No quarrel there."

Four

"**B**ut, Daddy, he's a *criminal*."

Louis Ellison gazed at his daughter over the rim of his reading glasses and let the Friday evening edition of the *Endicott Examiner* fall forgotten into his lap. Angie had seen that look from him before, on many, many occasions, all throughout her life. And it still made her shrink back in discomfort.

Her father had gazed at her in that way every time she'd come running home with some story about how she'd found dinosaur bones on Mr. Klondike's farm, or how she'd seen old Mrs. Slovak boiling eye of newt and horn of toad in her backyard, or how Angie knew for a fact that Freddy Barry's father was really a fugitive from justice who had slaughtered his first wife and kids along with the family cocker spaniel in Ocala.

Naturally, her father had never believed her. He hadn't then, and he didn't now. She could tell just by looking at him.

"Da-aa-dee-ee," she implored him, punctuating the plea with a shake of her whole body. "He *is*."

Her father frowned at her, dipping his head even lower, so that his gaze was more penetrating, and the light from the lamp beside him bounced off the shiny surface of his scalp. "Angela Delilah Ellison, I will not have you speak that way about a perfectly nice man."

"Perfectly nice man?" she repeated incredulously, nearly choking on the words. "Ethan Zorn is a low-life, scumbag, murdering slug who works for the mob."

Angie knew he was, because she had called Maury in Philadelphia, and he had assured her yet again that his information about Ethan Zorn was perfectly correct. She just hoped Maury knew what he was talking about.

Her father sighed with much feeling, gave the newspaper a vigorous shake and went back to perusing the scores of the high-school football games from that afternoon. "He's a sales rep for the Cokely Chemical Corporation," Louis said wearily from behind the rows of black-and-white columns. "And after meeting with him this afternoon, I'm halfway inclined to start an account with the company. Mr. Zorn offered me some very competitive terms and some very good incentives."

"Oh, sure," she said. "Fine. Go ahead and start an account with him. And just you wait. The next thing you know, you'll be waking up with a horse's head where Mom used to be."

"What was that, dear?" Her mother entered the living room then, right on cue. Millie Ellison's hands were covered with slightly singed oven mitts, her cheeks were as round and pink as persimmons, her salt-and-pepper hair was curling softly from the heat of the kitchen stove, and her ruffled apron was lovingly and indelibly dotted with years-old stains of butter and gravy and vegetable soup. She was, as far as Angie was concerned, Endicott's answer to June Cleaver.

Normally, Angie loved coming home on Friday nights, back to where she'd grown up, in the rambling Dutch colonial on Orchid Street furnished in traditional Norman Rockwell. She loved it number one, because she was such a lousy cook herself, and number two, because coming home usually centered her in times of stress. But not tonight. Not with her father taking sides with that…that…that low-life, scumbag, murdering slug Ethan Zorn.

"I said," Angie began again for her mother's benefit, "that if Daddy insists on doing business with mobsters, then he's going to find himself up to his tushie in horse's heads."

Her mother eyed her blankly. "Now, why would your father be doing business with mobsters? Louis, dear," she said to Angie's father, "are you doing business with mobsters and not telling me about it?"

Her father rattled the paper again and emitted a long growl of frustration. "Of course not, Millie. It's just Angie's wild imagination getting the better of her." Louis turned his attention to his daughter once more, throwing her a meaningful look. "Again."

"But—" Angie interjected.

"Ethan Zorn is a nice man," her father interrupted, "and he's here in town on legitimate business. He was so pleasant, in fact, that I thought you might like to meet him. I even invited him to—"

The melodious *ding-dong* of the front doorbell resonated through the living room then, and Louis Ellison rose eagerly from his chair to answer it. Angie watched him go, feeling a wide, sinking weight of dread settle at the very pit of her stomach. Oh, no, she thought as she spun away from the front door. Her father wouldn't. He couldn't. He didn't.

He did.

She heard Ethan Zorn's rich baritone erupt in greeting from behind her, and she slumped forward in defeat. She was going to be sharing her mother's famous Yankee pot roast at her parents' dinner table, with a criminal seated in the honored Guest Chair at her father's right-hand side. How much worse could her life get?

"Yeah, as a matter of fact, your daughter and I have already met," she heard the low-life, scumbag, murdering slug say from behind her. "It was the strangest thing. I came back from a business trip and found her in my—"

Her quick pivot around silenced him, but she could see that

he was smiling broadly. And dammit, he looked more handsome than ever, casually dressed in khaki trousers and a dark, pin-striped flannel shirt buttoned up over a navy blue T-shirt. He had rolled the long sleeves back to nearly his elbows, exposing well-defined forearms that no criminal deserved.

Angie met his gaze steadily and narrowed her eyes, then found herself wishing she'd thrown on something a little nicer than the blue jeans and nearly threadbare lightweight, white cotton sweater she was wearing. Her hair, too, was a mess, half in and half out of a ponytail that she hadn't bothered to tend since early afternoon.

He's a mobster, she reminded herself yet again, crossing her arms defensively over her waist. *What do you care what he thinks about your looks?* She returned his playful smile with what she hoped was an evil one of her own.

"Found her in your what?" her father asked, his expression puzzled and wary.

The question brought both Ethan's and Angie's attention back around. His grin turned smug. Hers turned pleading.

"In my...directory," Ethan told Louis. "The one the local chamber of commerce gave me identifying all the prominent people in town."

That surprised Angie enough to distract her for a moment. "I'm in a directory of prominent people in town? Really? I had no idea." Her smile grew genuinely warm. "That's so cool."

Louis Ellison's gaze wandered back and forth between the two of them, and Angie could see that he was more than a little interested in the byplay.

"Yes, you are," Ethan confirmed for her. "Under the heading of 'Local Media.'"

Angie arched her brows in mild surprise. "Well, how about that?"

She noticed then that Ethan Zorn was clutching a huge bouquet of multicolored chrysanthemums, and she blushed in spite of herself. He was contemptible, of course, but how sweet of him to bring her flowers. And in that mix of gold and orange that was her favorite color, too. How had he guessed? She smiled shyly and reached out her hand for them just as he turned to her mother.

"Mrs. Ellison," he said, extending the bouquet to Angie's mother, instead. "It's just my small way of saying thank you for your generosity in inviting me to dinner. It's not often a man who travels on business is treated to a home-cooked meal."

Hastily, Angie dropped her hand back to her side, but not before she noted Ethan's smirk.

This time her mother was the one to blush. "What a nice young man you are," Millie gushed, pulling off an oven mitt to take the flowers. She smiled at him with a smile that made her seem twenty years younger. Then she turned to throw her daughter a meaningful look. "How thoughtful. It's so uncommon to find such manners in young people today."

Angie refrained from comment, then spun around to march to the other side of the room. She heard her father invite Ethan to sit down, and quickly made her way to the Queen Anne chair by the fireplace so that she wouldn't wind up sharing the couch with her nemesis. But Ethan seemed not to notice, as he didn't even glance at the couch, but simply sat down in the other vacant chair. It was her father, she noted, who ended up on the sofa.

The two men exchanged pleasantries and talked business, and Angie had to admit as she listened to them that Ethan spoke as if he were exactly who he claimed to be. His knowledge of sales in general and the chemical industry in particular, along with the dialogue he shared with her father, appeared to be authentic and seemed very natural.

But hey, that didn't mean anything, she reminded herself. All kinds of people turned to a life of crime these days.

"So, Mr. Zorn," she said during a lull in the conversation, "I understand you're from Philadelphia."

He nodded. "Born and bred. I'm a South Philly boy through and through."

She nodded back. "I understand there's quite a lot of mob activity in the City of Brotherly Love."

"Angela…" her father cautioned her.

But Ethan only laughed good-naturedly. "There's a lot more to my hometown than crime, Miss Ellison. Sure, Philadelphia has its problems like any big city," he conceded with a shrug. "But I think you'd discover there's a lot to love there." He hesitated a telling moment before adding, "Maybe you'd like to come up for a visit sometime. It's a pretty exciting place. And I'd love to show you around."

"Oh, I just bet you would," she replied. He'd probably especially like to show her the Delaware River. Face first and with a concrete pylon tied to her ankle.

He opened his mouth to comment further, but Angie's mother sang out from the dining room, "Supper's ready."

The trio rose and made their way to the table, where they awkwardly volleyed for position. Angie, refusing to allow such a man the honor of sitting in the Guest Chair, tried to reach that seat first herself, but that's exactly where her father led Ethan at the same time. She and Louis tried to elbow each other out of the way for a full thirty seconds, but ultimately, Angie was forced to succumb to her father's superior strength and head-of-the-household status.

Grudgingly, she wound up plunking herself down directly opposite Ethan, in the chair her elder brother, James, occupied whenever he found time to break away from his professor of ichthyology position at Stanford. She wanted to keep as close an eye on their alleged guest as she possibly could. Her mother had set the table with the good silver, after all.

Surprisingly, except for a little mishap when Angie passed the gravy to Ethan—somehow, accidentally, of course, the gravy boat tipped forward and nearly emptied into his lap— dinner passed uneventfully. It was after dinner that things actually became eventful, beginning with Angie's mother's suggestion that Angie and Ethan take their coffee outside to enjoy it. On the patio. In the moonlight.

"It's a lovely evening," Millie remarked. "There are plenty

of stars in the sky. Maybe if you look hard enough, you'll be able to spot Bob, and then you can win the prize for first unaided sighting. I hear this year they're giving away a weekend at the Peek-a-Boo Inn on Lake Modoc,'' she sang out as an added incentive.

"It's too early to see the comet with the naked eye," Angie said, deciding not to dwell on the extremely odd fantasies about Ethan Zorn that erupted in her brain when the words "naked" and "Peek-a-Boo" were used so close together. "It'll be at least a few more days before Bob is close enough to spot."

Millie pinned her daughter with a pointed gaze. "Well, why don't you two go outside and look for him anyway?"

Great, Angie thought. Now her mother was trying to fix her up with the criminal element, too.

But instead of arguing, which she knew was pointless where her mother was concerned, Angie poured coffee into two of the delicate china cups and handed one to Ethan. She tried not to notice how oddly handsome he became when she considered the incongruity of such a huge, overwhelming man looking so comfortable cradling the frail little cup with the handpainted roses.

He'd probably snuffed out human lives with those very hands, she told herself. Yet he could cradle a teacup as easily as Queen Elizabeth did.

Then, without acknowledging him further, but certain he would follow her nonetheless—surely he wanted to prolong her agony with his very presence as long as he possibly could—Angie made her way to the back door and out into the fickle night air.

With the setting of the sun, the day had grown cooler, and with darkness fully descended, the night was downright cold. Unwillingly, Angie shivered, and felt Ethan move up close behind her.

"Cold?" he asked as he curled an arm around her waist and tugged her close against him.

She grasped her cup tighter and stepped away from him,

then strode to the edge of the patio. "I'm fine," she lied, reaching down to finger a late-blooming red zinnia nervously. Unfortunately, her body betrayed her with an uncontrolled quiver. She quickly and carefully sipped her coffee, but when the hot liquid did nothing to warm her or soothe her trembling, she began to understand that it was Ethan's nearness, and not the night air, that made her shiver so.

"You're not fine," he countered, his voice laced with humor. "You're freezing. Here."

He set his coffee cup on the ledge of the hip-high stone wall that surrounded the patio, then tugged his shirttail out of his trousers and began unbuttoning his flannel shirt. Angie watched the action with reluctant fascination, unable to say a word, because her voice was stuck somewhere in her throat.

He was getting undressed. For her. That's the only realization that entered her brain as she watched the nimble movement of his fingers from one button to the next. And all she could do was stand there wishing the circumstances were different, that instead of standing in her parents' backyard, they were back in Ethan's bedroom with Bob meddling in their affairs.

Against her quietly voiced objections, he shrugged out of his shirt and draped it over her shoulders before she could dart out of the way. Immediately, she was surrounded by the warmth and scent of him, something reminiscent of a slow desert sunrise. And without intending to, she found herself snuggling eagerly into the soft fabric and inhaling deeply.

"Thanks," she said quietly. "But now you're going to get cold."

He arched an eyebrow curiously as he pulled the long sleeves of his T-shirt down to his wrists. "Why, Miss Ellison. Don't tell me you're suddenly concerned about my welfare."

She lifted her coffee cup to her lips and breathed deeply the warm wisps of fragrant steam rising from it. "Let's just say I don't want you to freeze to death in my parents' backyard. I wouldn't want to see them wind up the target of a retaliatory mob hit."

He chuckled at that, then hoisted himself up to sit on the stone wall and picked up his coffee again. He studied her with much interest from over the rim of his cup, never saying a word, until Angie couldn't stand his silence any longer.

"What are you looking at?" she asked impatiently.

Immediately, he replied, "A woman with a very vivid imagination."

She sighed her exasperation. "So I've been told."

"Don't sound so disappointed," he told her. "A vivid imagination isn't such a bad thing."

"Oh, sure, easy for you to say. You probably never had to worry about inventing crazy scenarios to keep yourself interested in life when you were a kid. You grew up in Philadelphia. There was probably always something exciting going on in your neighborhood."

He was quiet for a moment, then asked, "Have you ever actually *been* anywhere other than Endicott?"

She frowned at him. "Of course I've been other places. I went to college in Bloomington, for Pete's sake."

He didn't even try to hide his amusement. "Oh, well, hey, you've been everywhere then, haven't you?"

"It's a nice place," she countered defensively.

"I don't doubt it for a minute."

"And I've been to Cincinnati a couple of times, too," she told him. "And Indianapolis." A little less vehemently, she added, "*And* I've been to Paris and Versailles, and Glasgow and London, Warsaw...Athens and Sparta, too."

That clearly surprised him. "You did the European tour thing?"

She glanced back down into her cup. "Um, no. Not exactly. It was, um...Paris, Kentucky, I visited. And...and Versailles, Kentucky." This time she pronounced "Versailles" with a decidedly less French pronunciation. "Glasgow and London, Kentucky. Warsaw, Kentucky. And, uh..." She cleared her throat indelicately. "Um, Athens and Sparta...Kentucky." She glanced back up apologetically. "I was doing a story for the paper back when I was on the travel beat. 'The Wonders

Down Under—Kentucky, Our European Neighbor To The South.'''

He laughed again. "So you really have been around."

"Maybe I haven't been as many places as you have," she told him, "but I'm not as naive as you seem to think I am, either. There's more to life experience than traveling."

"You're absolutely right," he concurred, surprising her. "Hey, travel is great, Angel—don't get me wrong. But I kind of like the fact that you've led such a sheltered life. Makes you more..."

She wasn't sure she wanted to know, especially when she considered the rough, uneven tone of voice he seemed to have suddenly adopted. But she found herself asking anyway. "More what?"

He glanced away, up toward the night sky, then dropped his gaze back down to his coffee. "More...pure," he said quietly. "That's all."

"Gee, just what I've always wanted to be," she muttered. "Pure. I thought that was supposed to be Kirby's label around town. Not that she hasn't *tried*...."

"Who's Kirby?"

Angie shook her head. "No one. Just a friend, that's all."

Ethan gazed at Angie the Angel, and even through the darkness, he could see that she was growing less antagonistic and more mellow. Funny, how the night did strange things to people, he thought. Funny, how it shadowed everything and highlighted nothing, so that whatever it enveloped—or whoever it enveloped—suddenly stood on equal footing. You could hide who you really were in the darkness, if only for a little while. And suddenly, Ethan wanted to do just that. Suddenly, he wanted to be someone else.

If only for a little while.

"Why are you being so nice to me all of a sudden?" he asked. "Why aren't you spitting and clawing the way you have been?"

She glanced up at the night sky, scanning it from one side to the other, as if she were looking for something. Finally, she turned to face him again and replied, "I could ask you the same question. Why are you being so nice to me and my family?"

He shrugged. "That's easy enough to answer. I like you, Angel. And I like your family, too."

"But you're after my family's livelihood."

He smiled cryptically. "Am I?"

"Yes. You are," she told him, though she was growing more and more uncertain of her conviction in that respect. "And not only that," she continued, "I have the ability to expose you for who you really are."

He smiled again. "Do you?"

She nodded, but the action was in no way confident.

He hesitated, wondering just how far he should carry this improvisational game they seemed to be playing. At last, he asked her, "And how are you planning to…expose me, as you so interestingly put it, for who I really am? For that matter, who am I? Really, I mean. Do you even know for sure?"

She dropped her gaze back into her cup. "I know who you are. Like I said, I have my—"

"Sources," he finished for her. "So you've said."

She snapped her head back to look at him, her expression decidedly less mellow now. But she uttered nothing to expand on her claim.

"But do you have any proof?" he continued. "Anything other than your own suspicions, and your own so-called sources, to back up your charge that I'm not who I claim to be?" When she returned her gaze silently and sullenly to the night sky, he nodded. "No, I didn't think you did."

"It's only a matter of time," she assured him. Then she looked at him again. "You're awfully chatty about this. You're actually talking to me as if you're coming clean about your true identity."

He feigned innocence. "Am I? I didn't mean to."

She narrowed her eyes at him. "So *are* you admitting that you're not who you claim to be?"

"I don't know. Am I?"

"You tell me."

He parted his lips fractionally, and eyed her curiously for a moment. "What if I'm *not* who I've been claiming to be?" he asked. "What if I'm not who you think I am? Would that change your feelings for me?"

She expelled a disgusted sound. "I don't have any feelings for you."

"Oh, now I know better than that, Angel. No woman responds to a man the way you respond to me unless she has feelings for him. Those feelings might not necessarily all be good, but you do have feelings for me."

"Dream on."

His voice turned warm as he responded, "I have been. Believe me. But my fantasies aren't the topic of discussion right now. We'll have plenty of time to get to those later." She started to say something to interrupt him, so he hurried on. "No, what we're talking about right now are your true feelings for me."

"I thought what we were talking about was your true identity."

"Were we? Okay, then, my true identity."

She eyed him warily. "Which is?"

He smiled again. "You're the newshound. You tell me."

She uttered a growl of frustration. "No, *you* tell *me*."

"Tell you what?"

"Why are you playing this game with me?" she demanded.

"Am I playing a game?"

"Why do you answer every question with another question?"

"Have I been doing that?"

"Haven't you?"

He shrugged, but said nothing, only continued to smile at her with what he hoped was an I-know-something-you-don't-know smugness. Because he did know something she didn't know. And he hoped like hell he was still around when she found out what it was.

Angie the Angel shook her head slowly and stared back up

at the sky. "Thanks, Bob," she said softly, her voice laced with disgust. "Thanks a lot. For nothing."

Ethan followed her gaze up toward the black, velvety night, his curiosity getting the better of him. "You got comets doing you favors, Angel?" he asked.

She laughed, a heartfelt, sarcastic sound. "Not likely. Damned comet. Making wishes come true. Who does he think he is?"

Ethan waited for her to elaborate, and when she didn't, he continued with their conversation himself. "So now that we've settled the topic of my true identity—"

"We have *not* settled that," she interrupted him.

"Then we can move along to that other topic," he concluded as if she hadn't spoken.

"What other topic?"

"That one where we talk about your true feelings for me. Which, as we both know, are pretty intense."

She turned her back on him, then moved slowly toward a darkened corner of the patio. He watched as she settled her cup on the wall and drew his shirt more closely around herself, crossing her arms over her midsection beneath it. Although her posture was anything but inviting, he leaped down from the wall and followed her to where she stood, placing his cup next to her cup as closely as he did his body next to hers.

"You're out of your mind," she said softly. "I don't have any feelings for you. Except bad ones."

He chuckled. "Yeah, I know how that is."

She said nothing in response to that, and he wished he could tell what she was thinking. So much about her suggested that what she kept insisting was true—that she was indeed utterly repelled by him. But there was *something*—he couldn't quite put his finger on exactly what—that made him think she wanted him to come closer. To touch her. To pull her into his arms. To kiss her as he had that first night in his bedroom.

Ethan had always lived dangerously, ever since he was a boy, and he'd always acted on his urges. Tonight was in no way different. So he did exactly what his instincts told him to do. He moved a step closer to Angie. He reached out a hand to slowly trace the elegant line of her jaw with his fingertip. He saw the pulse at the base of her throat leap and dance, then she turned to meet his gaze levelly.

Something in her eyes made her appear lost somehow, and suddenly, he wanted to help her find her way back to whatever it was she was seeking. So he curled his arm around her waist, turned her body to face his and dipped his head to kiss her.

What happened after that, he would never fully understand. Something inside him began to slowly unwind, as if he'd been pulled taut all his life and was finally able to ease. After years and years of running toward something he'd never quite been able to define—or perhaps running away from something, he wondered vaguely now—a feeling descended over him that he was finally, finally, exactly where he ought to be. Right where he belonged. Where he needed to remain forever.

So he kissed Angie again, brushing his lips gingerly over hers before tasting her more deeply. He drank of her sweetness, her succor, her sympathy, and found the sustenance he needed to survive for one more day.

Angie felt Ethan's kiss straight down to her toes, and could only marvel at the realization that something so obviously wrong could feel so wonderfully right. She forgot, for a moment, that Ethan Zorn was a dangerous man. Forgot, for a moment, that she should run away from him, not hurtle herself more eagerly into his embrace. Forgot, for a moment, that what she was doing was completely insane.

Instead, for a moment, she responded to the man, to the night, to the darkness, to the comet. Because she was certain that whatever was happening to her was all Bob's fault. Yes, it was a convenient excuse. But it was also a documented fact that Bob's approach to Endicott influenced the townsfolk greatly. Angie had never disbelieved that. And now she was experiencing for herself that it was true.

And what an experience to have for an illustration. Ethan's mouth on hers was warm and willing, wild and wonderful. The exquisite perfection of his passionate expertise quite overwhelmed her. He skimmed his fingertips along her jaw, tangled his hand in the unruly curls that had tumbled free of their binding and kissed her even harder. Only the need for breath tore her mouth from his, and the moment she had gulped that single gasp of air, he set upon her again.

This time when he kissed her, he dropped one hand to her waist and pulled her body flush against his. He splayed his hand open over the small of her back, urging her closer still, until she could feel the heated heart of him ripening against her belly. Her knees buckled beneath her at the realization that he was so ready, so rapidly, and he hooked his other arm around her shoulders to hold her steady.

The hand at her waist began to climb higher then, until his thumb and fingers lay open beneath the lower curve of her breast. Her heart leaped wildly behind her rib cage, drumming against her chest in an erratic tattoo. But instead of pulling away from him, as her rational mind insisted she do, Angie crowded her body closer to his, covered his hand with hers and cupped both over her breast.

A wild little cry escaped him, and he closed his fingers fully over her, rubbing the pad of his thumb across her nipple with the random savagery of a tropical storm. Angie moaned at the sensations rocking her with every eager caress of his hand. Wildly, she thrust her fingers into his hair to pull his head down to hers, and then she tried to devour him more completely. She lured his tongue into her mouth for a more thorough seduction, then scraped her fingernails along each of his ribs and around to the ripple of muscles along the length of his back.

He seemed to surround her. All she could feel, all she could smell, all she could taste was Ethan. His breathing was rapid and ragged, the heat from his body nearly blistering. No matter which way she moved, he was there, touching her, consuming her, savoring her. She felt his hands on her breasts, in her hair, curving possessively over her bottom, pulling her closer, ever closer, until she felt as if their bodies were fused as one forever.

In return, she explored him, every solid plane of muscle, every rigid cord of sinew, every fervid inch of flesh. And with every trip of her fingers, she fell more completely under his spell. He was no longer a man to be feared and avoided, and she was no longer a woman who was frightened and uncertain. He was simply a man, and she was a woman. And together, they generated magic.

Only when her own fingers wandered over the cool metal of his belt buckle did Angie slow her assault. She reminded herself she was in her parents' backyard. That the last time she'd been caught necking on the patio, she'd been grounded for a month. But oh… It would be worth an eternity of groundings if she could just have one more taste of Ethan Zorn.

Yet ultimately, it was he instead of she who ended the kiss. He jerked his head back from hers, panting at the interruption, his fingers flexing convulsively into her shoulders, even as he tried to move her to arm's length. Angie was too dazed, too delirious, to react right away, and could only wonder why she was suddenly so cold when she had just been so hot. Ethan towered over her, the breath leaving his mouth in a rapid rush of silvery fog, and those beautiful, benevolent brown eyes became almost bestial.

"What if I really am who you think I am?" he asked, his words rushed, anxious.

"What?" she replied dreamily, still focused on the meandering warmth that radiated throughout her body.

"What if I am in Endicott scoping out your father's company for an interested party that's…shall we say, anything but legitimate?"

The question brought Angie around with a start. "What are you trying to tell me?"

He stared at her in silence for a moment, his jaw clenched, but his fingers wandered idly into her hair. "What if I really am the threat you think I am?" he asked her softly.

She swallowed hard and tried not to dwell on the fact that she was clinging to him with all her might and had no desire to let him go. Ever. "Is this a confession?" She asked the

question so quietly she wasn't sure he was even able to hear
her.

He continued to hold her gaze steady as he said, "I need
to know, Angel."

"Know what?"

"If you really understand what's happening here."

She nodded, though her thoughts were vague and incoherent. "Of course I know. It's Bob."

Ethan shook his head slowly, his expression clearly confused. "Bob?" he asked. "The comet?"

She nodded again, with a bit more certainty this time. "He
does this kind of thing whenever he comes around."

"What kind of thing?"

"He messes with people. Makes them do things they
wouldn't normally do."

Ethan's expression fell. "Oh, Angel, you don't really buy
into all that hoodoo...do you?"

This time her nod was vehement. "You bet I do. I've seen
it happen. Perfectly normal people doing the dumbest things.
All because of Bob."

"Oh, sure. Blame it on Bob," Ethan spat. "That's so convenient. Throw caution to the wind, do something wild and
impulsive that you wouldn't usually do, enjoy it immensely,
then explain it away as being all Bob's fault."

"No, that's not it at all," Angie objected. "It's some kind
of galactic disturbance or something. Whenever Bob comes
within a certain number of miles of Endicott, he starts affecting people's personalities. It's a documented fact."

"Who documented it?"

She shrugged. "I don't know. Some scientists, I guess.
Bob's unexplainable activities have always driven the scientific community crazy."

When she realized she was still clutching Ethan with a pos-
sessiveness to rival any lover's, she forced her fingers to un-
curl, made herself take a step backward, compelled herself to
look away. "I mean," she added nervously, "you can't possibly think *I* would be standing out here in the moonlight kiss-

ing a man like *you* if it wasn't for some kind of cosmic interference.''

When he didn't answer her, she braved a glance back at him again. He stood with his hands settled menacingly on his hips and his teeth clenched, his expression one of obvious resentment. ''Oh, can't I?'' he said.

But before she could reply, he marched toward her, jerked his shirt from her shoulders and shrugged into it once more. His gaze never left hers as he buttoned himself up again and stuffed his shirttail back into his trousers.

''Good night, Miss Ellison,'' he said stiffly. ''Please extend my apologies to your parents for taking off without a word like this. I'm not feeling so good all of a sudden. And do give them my thanks,'' he added as he turned away. ''It's been a real pleasure.''

And with that, he was gone, disappearing into the night like a shadow. Angie turned her gaze upward, toward the night sky. She cursed the comet for being so damned predictable, and wondered what on earth she could possibly do to halt the onslaught of bizarre feelings she'd been experiencing for Ethan Zorn.

Okay, so he was definitely something exciting, exactly what she had wished for fifteen years ago. But comet or no comet, she had to get ahold of herself. The man was bad news. Period. For her. For her family. For the entire population of Endicott. Somehow, she had to make sure everyone knew that. And somehow, she had to make sure she never fell under his spell again.

''Oh, sure, Angie,'' she mumbled. ''And just how are you going to manage that?''

Above her, way off in the distance, a lone star, brighter than the rest, winked and twinkled brighter. And somehow, even though it was way too early for him to be around, she just knew it was Bob, laughing at her.

Five

She'd gone too far.

Ethan shook his head in disbelief at the byline on the teeny-tiny, almost invisible article, buried on the lower left-hand corner of page six of the *Endicott Examiner*'s "About Town" section. *Crime Comes To Endicott?* the headline read in bold-face type, however small. Beneath it were the words *Angela Ellison, Crime Beat.*

Well, at least she had worded it in the form of a question, he thought with some disgust. Great. This was just great. After everything the two of them had shared, she'd gone and ambushed him. He should have tied her up when he'd had the chance.

The phone on his nightstand rang shrilly behind him, jarring him out of his reverie and into reality, which he had to admit was the last place he wanted to be at the moment. Snatching up his suit jacket and curling his fingers convulsively around the handle of his briefcase, he rushed from the bedroom, pretending he hadn't heard the phone. He raced down the stairs and out into the sunny September morning, ignoring the ring of the phone in his office, as well.

Let Mrs. Mack handle it, he thought. Between her bad hearing, worse handwriting and Palmieri's outrage at the situation, Ethan would have a good excuse for why he hadn't been able to make heads or tails of the ensuing messages he was sure would meet him when he returned home tonight.

If he returned home tonight. He still wasn't sure just how serious a threat the big boys were going to consider this whole thing.

He slammed his car door with more force than was necessary, rocking the little red Porsche as if it were nothing more than a ladybug. Then he ground the engine to life and stomped the accelerator a few times, pretending to have Angela Ellison, Crime Beat, in his sights. She couldn't possibly imagine what she'd just done to seal her fate. And his, too, for that matter. He had his work cut out for him if he had a hope in hell of setting things straight now.

Yeah, he thought further as he threw the car into gear and squealed away from the curb, he really should have tied her up when he'd had the chance.

Angie was sitting at her desk, munching absently on a chicken-salad sandwich and reading a spy thriller, when a huge fist slammed down on her desk within millimeters of her diet soda. She jumped in her chair, nearly toppling it backward. Then she glanced up, ready to fire both barrels at whatever imbecile had startled her in such a way, and found herself nearly eye to eye with a *very* angry Ethan Zorn.

"What the hell were you thinking to publish a piece of garbage like this?" he demanded, thrusting that morning's edition of the *Examiner* under her nose.

Angie pushed back her chair and stood, setting her lunch gingerly on her desk. She brushed her palms together to rid them of crumbs before swiping her hands over her navy, pin-striped trouser legs to dry the sweat she felt forming there.

She tugged indelicately at the collar of her navy blue blouse and strove for command of her voice before speaking.

"Actually," she said, cursing the squeaky little sound that emerged from her mouth, "if you want to get technical, it wasn't *me* who published that piece of—" She stopped herself quickly, cleared her throat and tried again. "Who published that article," she corrected herself. "It was my editor. Marlene. I'm just the person who wrote it, that's all."

His dark eyes turbulent, Ethan glared at her. "Then what the hell were you thinking to *write* a piece of garbage like this?"

Angie lifted her chin defiantly. "It's not garbage. It's a solid article."

He cast the offending newspaper down on her desk and settled his hands firmly on his hips in challenge. "It's yellow journalism is what it is."

She gaped at him, outraged. "It is not. We at the *Examiner* print only the facts as we see them."

He shook his head at her in what she could only liken to disappointment. "As you see them," he muttered, clearly disgusted. "I guess I should be grateful that you didn't actually name any names." He seemed to relent some then, and added, "Actually, I guess I should be grateful that the article says pretty much nothing about anything."

"Hey!" she interrupted him indignantly in defense of her work, despite the fact that she knew he was right. Marlene had edited down and watered down Angie's story until it was little more than a collection of words that said, well…pretty much nothing about anything.

"But you're playing with fire here, Angel," Ethan cautioned her. "You have no idea what you're doing. What you've already done. And I'm telling you right now, for your own good. Back off."

Oh, now *that* was a threat, she thought, no two ways about it. Angie glanced around the newsroom and noted much to her dismay that she was thoroughly and utterly alone. There were only nine people on the newspaper's staff, and all of them, except her, generally went home for lunch. She, being the newshound that she was, preferred to stay at the office and man the phones. Fruitlessly, on most days, because no one ever called in any news. Today, however, Angie had yet another reason to regret staying on board alone.

"You're just trying to intimidate me," she said softly.

Ethan Zorn flattened both palms on her desk and leaned down to push his face directly in front of hers. "Yeah, you're damned right I am."

She swallowed hard. "Well, it's not going to work. I'm sticking by my story. You're a criminal, and you're trying to bring organized crime to this community, and I'm going to expose it and you." She crossed her arms over her chest and added, "It's my moral and civic duty."

Ethan chuckled, a sound that was in no way jovial. "Angel, you get any closer to what you think is a story, and you're going to create a lot of problems for a lot of people. Not the least of which is you."

"I'm not afraid of you," she vowed, her voice small and quiet and completely insecure.

He smiled. A big, menacing, vicious smile. "The hell you're not."

"I'm not," she insisted. She'd kissed him, after all. Twice. How could she still be afraid of him? Of course, she reasoned, there was still the distinct possibility that he was a complete sociopath. But then, nobody was perfect, right?

His gaze never left hers. "We'll see about that." He pushed himself away from her desk and stood, straightening his necktie and his jacket. "Pull another stunt like this one, Angel, and it's going to cost you."

She exhaled a breath she hadn't been aware of holding, then tried to force her body to relax. "Says you," she retorted maturely.

"Yeah, says me," he assured her. "And a couple of other interested parties."

Well, that certainly caught her attention. Maybe she could draw him out a little. "Oh?" she asked, her hard nose for news finally kicking in to shove aside the mousy little woman in jeopardy. "Like who?"

His smile turned feral and he answered as maturely as she had a moment ago, "That's for me to know and you to find out."

She smiled back, with every bit as much calculation. "And I will find out. I promise you that."

He shook his head slowly. "Just don't make me say this twice, okay? Because the next time, I might not be so polite. If you get my drift."

She gaped at him. "You *are* threatening me, aren't you?"

In reply to her charge, he casually unbuttoned his jacket. When the garment fell open, her gaze was drawn immediately to the big gun holstered over his rib cage. "No threat, Angel," he said in a low, level voice. "Just a cautionary advisory. I'd hate to see anything happen to a nice, clean-cut girl like you."

"Oh, yeah, I just bet you would."

"I would. It's not every day that a man like me is admired from afar by a sweet, pure thing like you."

She felt herself blush at that, the warm rush of blood igniting beneath her fair skin like a wildfire on dry brush.

"Then again," he purred, "you've been bringing your...admiration closer and closer lately, haven't you?"

Oh, he *would* bring up that little incident of three nights ago on her parents' patio, wouldn't he? she thought. She was about to toss off some retaliatory remark, but before she could utter anything in response, Ethan Zorn spoke again.

"Watch your back, Angel," he told her. "Not everybody in my line of work is as reasonable as I am."

"And which line of work would that be, Mr. Zorn? Are we talking about your gig as a sales representative for the Cokely Chemical Corporation? Or your wise-guy status with the mob?"

He grinned at her with much indulgence. "Look at it this way," he said evenly. "Either you're going to wind up with a libel suit on your hands, or you're going to wind up in a cement overcoat. Either way, you got problems, you know what I'm saying?''

Then, without further notice, he pivoted around and strode casually across the newsroom and out the door, as if their odd, electrically charged exchange had never occurred.

Angie nibbled her lip as she eyed the door through which he'd exited, seeing something else entirely. Boy, he had some nerve. After everything the two of them had shared together, he still had the audacity to threaten her. Well, he was about to find out that Angela Ellison, Crime Beat, didn't scare easily. Her mind began to buzz with a follow-up story to her morning article. She glanced at the clock. If she hurried, she just might be able to make the evening edition....

It was already dark when Angie arrived home the following evening, and she was exhausted from defending her follow-up story in the *Examiner* all day. Every fine, upstanding citizen in Endicott had telephoned or stopped by the paper, demanding to know the meaning of her articles. Crime comes to Endicott? Why, it was unthinkable. Angie had spent half of her time trying to explain why she'd written the stories, and the other half trying to explain what they were about.

And it was with only a fleeting feeling of uncertainty that she hoped once again she'd managed to get all her facts for the two stories straight.

Of course she'd gotten her facts straight, she assured herself as she shoved her key into the lock of her front door and twisted it. Just because she didn't actually have those facts in writing—yet—to substantiate all the claims she'd made about Ethan Zorn's ''business'' in town, that wasn't so terrible, was it? She knew what he was up to, even if no one else would believe it.

She had her sources, after all. Well, one source anyway. Maury. A friend of hers from college, a fellow journalism major who now worked for none other than the *Philadelphia Inquirer*. He'd investigated the death of a Philadelphia mob boss a month ago, and he'd alerted Angie when the name of her hometown kept cropping up in some pretty suspicious places.

Maury had made a deal with her: if she wanted to follow up on the story at her end, he'd stay on top of things at his. The two of them could share information, and eventually, they'd blow the story sky-high.

Okay, so Maury worked the obituaries for the *Inquirer* and had done the sleuthing during his lunch breaks with absolutely no sanctioning from the paper. He was still a legitimate, reliable source, she told herself. Pretty much. At any rate, Angie was sticking by her stories.

Besides, it wasn't as though she had actually *named* Ethan Zorn in either of the articles, she reminded herself as she pushed her front door open and gathered her mail up from the floor beneath the mail slot. Or anyone else, for that matter. She frowned as she sifted through the assortment of bills and advertisements.

Okay, so both stories had basically said nothing at all about anybody or anything, she conceded with a sigh of frustration. Mostly all they'd done was confuse the entire population of Endicott—and right when the Comet Festival was getting into full swing, too, the mayor had reminded her. Angie would have time to fill in the gaps and cite all her information in the future. She had *lots* of follow-up stories planned, after all.

She had taken three steps into her living room, had dropped her keys back into her purse and had tossed her mail onto the desk by the front door before she realized something was wrong. She glanced up warily, narrowing her eyes in suspicion. She always left the much brighter green lamp by the couch on when she went to work in the morning, not the standing brass lamp in the corner that offered little more than a pale yellow glow.

And she was absolutely certain she had turned the radio off before leaving. In any case, she always listened to the news channel during her morning preparations, not the jazz station. But the music that greeted her now was muted and low, a bluesy, heartfelt rendition of "Don't Get Around Much Any-more" on tenor sax.

Then the front door crashed shut behind her, and Angie spun abruptly around to find that she wasn't alone. Ethan Zorn was leaning against the wall gazing back at her, wearing a *very* disturbing expression, one that made him seem altogether too big and too vicious. At exactly the same time Angie opened her mouth to scream, Ethan casually flipped open his suit jacket to reveal his very big, very vicious gun, tucked into its leather shoulder holster. With much reluctance, she snapped her mouth shut again.

Ethan grinned, his perfect white teeth and expensively tailored suit at odds with his menacing posture. When her heart began to hammer hard in her chest, she squeezed her eyes shut. He'd kissed her, she reminded herself. Really tenderly, too. He couldn't possibly hurt her after they'd shared something like that. Could he? Unless of course... Well, there was still that potential sociopath business that had her wondering.

"Angel," he greeted her, his voice low and as smooth as ages-old cognac. "You and I need to have a little chat."

Angie had no idea how to react. She tried to remind herself that he was probably dangerous—just about anyone who broke into someone else's home would be, she supposed, choosing to ignore that she had done just that herself not too long ago. But certainly Ethan Zorn seemed less likely to do her harm than, say, that creepy bag boy at the grocery store who always seemed to handle her grapefruits a tad suspiciously.

So instead of reacting, Angie stood in place, watching Ethan and waiting. Waiting to see what he would do next. Waiting to hear what he might have to say to explain his uninvited presence in her home. Waiting to see if maybe the building would go up in fortuitous flames.

When he only continued to stand in place and watch her in return, Angie shifted her weight from one foot to the other and tried to remember if she had stashed anything in the living room that she might use for a weapon, just in case he *had* sort of conveniently forgotten about those two heart-melting kisses.

But unless she was suddenly able to rouse the strength to wield a Barc-o-Lounger, she was out of luck.

"Oh?" she finally responded, uncertain whether the soft utterance even escaped her lips.

Ethan nodded. "Oh, yeah."

"A-a-about what?" she managed to say with only a minor stammer, cursing herself for even that show of nervousness.

Ethan shoved himself away from the wall, pushed the front door shut completely and turned the dead bolt with an ominous *click*. Then he spun around to face Angie, still looking vicious and menacing, and in nothing close to a good mood. He strode slowly toward her and didn't stop until the toes of his expensive Italian loafers connected to her Payless specials.

Then he bent forward until his forehead was nearly touching hers and said, "About how you're really becoming a pain in the butt."

Okay, gun or no gun, that really made her mad. "*I'm* a pain in the butt?" she repeated, lifting herself up on tiptoe in an effort to get in his face this time. "Hey, I'm not the one who's trying to shake down this town, pal. You are."

He actually smiled at that. Well, not exactly a smile, Angie had to amend. But one corner of his mouth did lift into something of a smile. Sort of. Okay, a twitch, but it was something.

"Shake down this town?" he echoed. "Do you honestly think that's the way we talk?"

"So you're finally admitting you're connected?" she asked, half-fearful of his response.

He shook his head silently, a gesture that really told her nothing at all. "I think I need a drink," he said suddenly. As casually as he had approached her, he now wandered away. "Where do you keep the bar?" he asked, as if all people kept a nice, neat little cocktail area in their home.

"There's some wine in the fridge," Angie volunteered, wondering idly why she bothered. It wasn't as though she had any desire to actually entertain a felon in her home.

Instantly, Ethan spun around to prowl toward the little galley kitchen that was clearly visible from the front door. Within moments, he returned to the living room, clutching a glass in each hand, both half filled with something dark red. When he handed one to Angie, she sipped it without thinking, hoping the mellow liquid might do something to ease her trembling. Immediately after she'd completed the action, however, it occurred to her in a wild rush of fancy that her uninvited guest had had the opportunity to drug the wine, and she spit the mouthful she had consumed back into the glass.

"I know," Ethan said with an understanding nod. "It's awful, isn't it? Frankly, your taste in wine stinks. Here's a good tip for starters, though—do *not* refrigerate red wine."

When she said nothing in response, but simply continued to stare at him, feeling more and more confused by the moment, he shrugged a bit and conceded, "Okay, Beaujolais *maybe* is fine to refrigerate. You want to serve that a little on the cool side. But burgundy, Angel." He shook his head and made a soft *tsk*ing sound. "We're talking full-bodied here. Room temperature."

She rolled her shoulders, a defensive gesture, and tried not to ponder the bizarre nature of her current predicament—receiving a wine lesson from a criminal. "But I like to drink red wine cold," she told him. "And Rosemary and Kirby always make fun of me when I put ice in it."

He flinched and squeezed his eyes shut tight, as if she had just slapped him, but he said nothing more. Instead he only sipped his wine, flinching again before swallowing.

"How did you get in here?" she demanded when she remembered that he was an uninvited guest. "I've been locking this place up tight every morning."

Ethan nodded. "Yeah, well, seeing as how I've been reading in the paper that there's a crime wave going on in this town, I'm not surprised."

She ignored his sarcasm and repeated, "How did you get in?"

Instead of giving her an immediate answer, he moved to her couch and set his wine on the coffee table before him. He glanced back up at Angie, then patted the cushion next to him in silent invitation. She moved slowly to stand before him, placed her glass on the table next to his, then pointedly seated herself in a bentwood rocker on the other side of the room.

Ethan dipped his head forward in silent acknowledgment of her gesture, then told her, "Here's another bit of advice—"

"Oh, you're just full of *it* today, aren't you?" Angie interrupted him.

"Never buy your locks from mom-and-pop-type hardware stores," he concluded as if she hadn't spoken. "Any lowlife could get into this place. You're just lucky I happened by before any lowlife did."

"Until you came to town, lowlife didn't exist in Endicott," she muttered, not quite under her breath.

The expression he threw her in response was puzzling—had she not known better, she would have thought she'd hurt his feelings with her comment. A funny heat began to burn through her midsection, and she fancied she could actually feel her blood zinging through her veins.

But her physical reaction wasn't a result of fear, she realized much to her irritation. No, the odd frisson of sensation winding through her now was one she unfortunately recognized easily enough. And simply put, at the moment, with his dark good looks, his overpowering presence and his rich, rousing voice, instead of frightening or intimidating Angie, Ethan Zorn was turning her on.

"Look," she began softly, trying to ignore the realization until she could better deal with it. "I know you're kind of peeved about the stories in the paper—"

"Kind of peeved?" he echoed incredulously. "Kind of *peeved?*"

"But, you know," she went on hastily, "really, they weren't nearly as bad as they could have been. When you get right down to it, they were really very…"

Ethan's grin—so warm, so welcoming, so void of anything evil or threatening—caught her off guard, and she immediately ceased rattling off whatever lame excuse had been about to tumble from her mouth. Instead, she could only gaze at him in silence, and marvel yet again at how it was such a shame that such a gorgeous guy had turned to a life of crime. He just didn't seem like a low-life, scumbag, murdering slug. On the contrary, he seemed like a really nice guy she'd like to get to know better.

"Who *are* you?" she heard herself mutter, uncertain when she had decided to voice the question aloud.

"Oh, come on, Angel. You know who I am," he said knowingly.

She nibbled her lip cautiously. "No, I don't think I do," she said with a soft sigh. "I thought I did, but now I'm not so sure. That's the problem. The latest one, anyway."

His smile in response to her dilemma was enigmatic, a combination of disappointment and satisfaction. "I'm Ethan Zorn," he said in a matter-of-fact manner that made her feel as if she were just meeting him for the first time. "A hard-working, hard-traveling, um…businessman. And since coming to your fair community, I suddenly find myself in a situation unlike anything I've ever experienced."

"Oh?" Angie asked. "And what situation would that be?"

His hesitation was slight, but she noted it nonetheless. Then he told her, "I suddenly find myself falling for a woman who thinks I'm something I'm not."

When he began to move slowly toward her, Angie swallowed hard. She told herself to say something, anything, because the conversation was beginning to take a *very* strange turn. But try as she might, she could spur nothing to move out of her brain and into her mouth. So she simply watched helplessly as Ethan drew nearer, growing larger and more dominating with every step he took forward.

"A woman," he continued in that maddeningly smooth voice, "who has professed to have been admiring me from afar for some time."

She opened her mouth to say something, but couldn't think of a single thing to stop the oncoming of what she was certain was something she did *not* want to hear.

"A woman," he went on, "with whom I've experienced…magic…twice now."

"I told you," Angie interjected, her voice scarcely audible, "that was just because of Bob. Any other time, I *never* would have—"

"Oh, yes, you would."

Ethan halted in front of her, looking down at her as if he were straddling Mount Olympus. His eyes met hers, then his gaze dipped lower, to her mouth, her neck, her breasts, her legs.

Somewhat self-consciously, she lifted a hand to the collar of her shirt and tugged it more snugly around her throat. The action only made his smile grow broader. Unable to tolerate his position of authority any longer, she slowly stood, then realized that standing up somehow only made her feel that much more vulnerable.

At least sitting down, she'd had an excuse for why he was so much larger than she was. Standing, and seeing that he was still so much larger than she was, she simply had to admit that he was a big, brawny guy, fully capable of overwhelming her if he so chose.

If he so chose, she repeated to herself. That was a good one. Choice had nothing to do with it. The fact was, Ethan Zorn was simply an overwhelming, overpowering man. A man who could take whatever he wanted, whenever he wanted it. So why was he playing with her the way he clearly was? What was the game with him? Why didn't he just do whatever it was mobsters did to innocent women and get it over with? Why did he want to make her crazy trying to second-guess him?

"So I say," he continued softly, "since we're both obviously more than a little interested in each other, then maybe we should just carry this thing to its logical conclusion."

"What do you want from me?" Angie heard herself ask then, her voice low and trembling and nothing at all like how she had hoped to project it.

He lifted a hand and curled his index finger under her chin, then brushed the backs of his knuckles gingerly over her mouth and up along her cheek. A burst of heat followed his touch, and a wild rush of energy sped through her entire body. Her eyes fluttered closed for only a moment, then she remembered who this man was and what he stood for. She forced herself not to be moved by his innocent, tender gesture—no easy feat, that—and did her best to glare at him.

"What do you want?" she repeated.

He cupped her jaw fully in his palm then, and stared straight into her eyes. "I want more than I could ever hope to have," he told her softly, cryptically. "But I'll settle for one or two other things, instead."

She shook her head slowly, an action that resulted in her face being even more intimately framed by his rough hand. "I don't understand," she told him.

He nodded, a gesture so slow and intent that she almost didn't notice it. "Yeah, I'm not sure I do, either, Angel."

She opened her mouth and was about to ask him something else, but he cut her off by dropping his hand to his side and taking a step backward. He returned to the coffee table, lifted both of their glasses of wine and downed his in one long series of swallows. He grimaced a bit, then strode back across the room to hand Angie her glass.

When she shook her head in refusal, he told her, "You better take it. You're gonna need it."

Although reason dictated she decline, she found herself reaching out to take the glass he extended. But instead of tasting the wine, she only reiterated, "Tell me. What is it you want from me?"

He continued to gaze at her for a moment, then cocked his head as if he were carefully contemplating both her and what he was about to tell her. Finally, in a soft, cajoling voice, he said, "I want you to help me choose a date. One that's mutually agreeable to us both. The sooner, the better."

Angie shook her head slightly, hoping to shake off the buzzing noise that had suddenly begun to vibrate between her ears. Her fingers convulsed on the stem of her wineglass as she asked a little breathlessly, "A date? What are you talking about?"

"For our wedding," Ethan told her.

She touched the tip of her tongue to the backs of her front teeth, and gave herself a moment to evaluate his statement. "Our wedding," she finally echoed, certain she must have misunderstood. The ringing in her head, after all, was growing more pronounced with every passing second. "You're asking me to marry you?"

He lifted his hand to her face again, the pad of his thumb grazing her cheek so gently it made her want to cry. "Angel," he said, his voice low and level and utterly serious, "I'm gonna make you an offer you can't refuse."

Six

Ethan wasn't sure he liked the expression on Angie's face, especially when it suddenly changed drastically. Until he'd announced his offer, she had been studying him with an odd, rather wary expression—as if he were some kind of tumor under a microscope she couldn't decide was malignant or benign.

Then, suddenly, she brightened, smiling the most sparkling smile he'd ever seen. In her baggy white, long-sleeved blouse and brown twill trousers, with her well-scrubbed demeanor and gee-whiz good looks, she seemed almost like a high-school kid who'd just been elected class president.

Except that no high-school kid had ever been able to send Ethan's blood racing through his body the way Angie Ellison seemed capable of doing with just a single glance his way.

"You're offering me a wedding?" she asked in a bright voice that immediately roused his suspicions. She snapped her fingers merrily and asked, "Just like that?"

He nodded, still feeling wary. "Just like that. Like I said...I've sort of fallen for you."

"You've fallen for me? Like love at first sight?" she chirped further, sounding way too agreeable about the discovery.

He nodded again, more slowly. "Yeah..."

"And now you want me to marry you?" she asked with a smile that nearly blinded him.

He nodded again, a bit less certainly this time. "Yeah..." he repeated, his voice trailing off.

"But gosh, Mr. Zorn," she gushed in much the same way a recently crowned prom queen would, "what if I don't want to get married?" After a moment spent dazzling him even more with her smile, she added breezily, "Especially to a low-life, scumbag, murdering slug like you?"

He narrowed his eyes at her. "Oh, you'll marry me," he assured her through gritted teeth. "Once you hear what I have to say."

She pouted like a debutante. "Oh, darn. And here I've been saving myself for Prince Edward."

"Sit down, Angel," Ethan instructed, jabbing a finger toward the couch. "Over there." He extended her still-full wineglass toward her with silent intent.

He had expected an argument from her, but to his surprise, she reacted exactly as he told her. She plucked the glass from his hand and strode purposefully toward the couch, then slumped into it and stared blindly down into her wine.

Ethan had gone around and around with the problem of Angie the Angel for two days now, and every time he'd pondered the dilemma, he'd always had no choice but to arrive at the same conclusion. The request for her imminent disappearance was coming at him from two sides, after all. And Ethan honestly wasn't sure which repercussions he feared more.

He didn't know how she'd managed to do it, because he'd been covering his tracks from the moment he'd left his home in Philadelphia. But Angela Ellison, ace reporter for the little, twice-daily *Endicott Examiner* had managed to blow open wide the story of the century, as far as this small town was concerned.

Obviously, Ethan and his colleagues had grossly underestimated the local citizenry when they'd decided to establish operations in southern Indiana. The Endicotians weren't quite as ill-informed as he and the others had assumed, nor were they as willing to roll over and play dead as he and the others had planned.

And now a nice girl like Angie Ellison had landed right in the thick of things. Somehow, she'd planted the seed in her head that she was going to save her hometown, the Midwest equivalent of Brigadoon, by bringing the mob to its knees and exposing it to the light of day.

Ethan shook his head slowly. He hated it when decent people got caught up in this kind of stuff. Because most of the guys he worked with weren't nearly as tender-hearted as he was himself when it came to disposing of people who meddled where they had no business meddling. If Ethan didn't do something to quiet Angie, then someone else would. And that someone else might just try to shut her up but good. At best, they'd launch a fear campaign against her, and terrify her into backing off her investigation. At worst, they'd rough her up. Bad.

Ethan didn't scare easily, but the guys he'd been playing with lately were wild cards. In spite of having been a member of their inner circle for six months now, he knew they still didn't trust him. And he sure as hell didn't trust them. Not where his own safety was concerned, and certainly not with Angie's.

She had insinuated just enough in her newspaper articles to set off alarms with virtually everyone Ethan had been working so hard to lure in. She'd suggested just enough to get the right people feeling the wrong way.

Man, mobsters were a paranoid bunch.

The only way Ethan knew to keep her safe and make sure the big boys didn't get their grubby hands on her was to offer her around-the-clock protection, and to establish her as someone who would remain ever true to him and his…occupation. And there was only one way he knew to do that.

He was going to have to marry the girl.

Call him old-fashioned, call him a sexist pig, call him crazy. He still liked to think of himself as something of a knight, however tarnished his armor had become over the years. And the fact was, even when he was running with the wrong crowd, a guy had to have some morals. A guy had to know where to draw the line between right and wrong.

Okay, so maybe Ethan's line had jumped around a lot in the past few years, but at least he still had a line. And making sure innocent people didn't get hurt was definitely on the right side of that line. But it was essential that in protecting Angie, he not raise anyone's suspicions about why she might need protecting. He had to have some legitimate excuse to be, in effect, living with her, so the locals wouldn't get suspicious.

Because, hey, this was Endicott, Indiana. Last of the small-time small towns. Hell, he wouldn't be surprised to find out there were thirty-year-old virgins living here. No morally upstanding woman like Angie Ellison was going to allow herself to be swept away by the likes of him. Not unless there was some kind of cosmic motivator she could conveniently blame—like Bob, for instance—and not without there being some kind of socially acceptable arrangement attached to the whole thing. Even if that arrangement was essentially against her will.

Ethan had no choice, and neither did Angie. He'd come to the only conclusion that made any sense, and he had to make her understand that. Simply put, he was going to have to marry her.

Or at least make the big boys—and everyone else in town—*think* he'd married her.

With much reluctance, he moved away from her, making his way slowly toward the living-room window. A small, inexpensive telescope sat precariously on a tripod beside it, and Ethan approached it with genuine interest.

"You have a telescope," he said, deliberately sidetracking

them from the subject at hand. Asking a woman for her hand in marriage—or rather, demanding it—wasn't something he wanted to rush into, after all.

He felt her hesitation from behind him, but she finally replied quietly, "Everyone in Endicott has a telescope when Bob comes around."

Ethan nodded, then bent to look through the eyepiece. "Can't see much," he said.

"I can see enough to know what's what."

Her comment brought his head back up, and he eyed her with interest. "I think, Angel, you only see the things you wanna see."

She narrowed her eyes at him, though whether in curiosity or suspicion, he had no idea. Then she stood up and set her wineglass on the coffee table, rounding it deftly to meet his gaze. "Is that so?" she asked, crossing her arms defensively over her midsection. "Well, as much as I'd love to meet Mr. Right and get married, I can see very clearly that you don't have what it takes, Mr. Zorn. Whatever wedding you're talking about, it won't include me."

He smiled. "We'll see about that."

He released the telescope and approached her again, but this time he stopped several inches before reaching her, tucking his hands into the pockets of his trousers. For a moment, he only gazed at her, at the dark, bottomless brown of her eyes, at the lips slightly parted as if in invitation, at the pink glow on her cheeks that told him she wasn't nearly as calm or careless as she was letting on. Then he strode negligently past her and pivoted around.

From the back, she was even more intriguing, he noted, all curves and softness that beckoned him to reach out and explore. And who knew—maybe that could come later, he told himself. Once they were "officially" man and wife. He supposed that part of it, at least where Angie was concerned, was up to Bob.

"Angel," he finally began again, adopting his very best Marlon Brando voice, "you've been sayin' some things around town that don't make me and my business associates look so good.''

She spun around at his comment and snarled at him. Actually snarled. ''Gee, Mr. Zorn, maybe that's because you and your *business associates* are a bunch of low-life, scumbag, murdering slugs—did you ever stop to think about that? And it's kind of hard to make a bunch of low-life, scumbag, murdering slugs look *good.*''

''Ooo, so the angel knows how to roar,'' Ethan said with a smile, tamping down his admiration that she could still spit and hiss and bare her claws—however ineffectually—when she was clearly cornered. He had to admit her bravado was moving. Stupid, but moving.

Very softly, she said, ''Like I told you yesterday, you don't scare me.''

He took a few steps toward her again, lowering his head and bending forward until he was nose to nose with her. Then he lifted his hand to her hair and wound a few dark blond curls around his index finger. ''Then maybe I'm just going to have to try a different tack.''

Her eyes widened at his suggestion, her pupils expanding to nearly the edge of the coffee-colored irises. ''No, that won't be necessary,'' she said, her voice softer now, more compliant. ''I'll listen to whatever it is you have to say.''

Her sudden capitulation unnerved him, but he decided to roll with it for now. Slowly, he released her hair again, then, hesitating for only a moment, moved back to stand in front of the couch. For some reason, putting distance between them seemed like a very good idea all of a sudden.

''Like I said,'' he began again, ''you've been spreading the word around town that I'm not to be trusted, that I'm here under pretenses other than what I described at our initial meeting. You remember that meeting, don't you, Angel?'' he added, just because he wanted to see her squirm. ''That night you asked me to tie you up?''

''I did *not*—''

''And I don't appreciate your insinuation that I'm not who

I say I am,'' he interrupted before she had the chance to object. He paused a telling beat, waiting until she met his gaze eye to eye. Then he added deftly, "Even if you are right about me. Even if I'm not who I say I am."

She opened her mouth to argue, then hastily closed it again and stared at him. "What?" she finally said.

"I said you're right about me."

"I am?"

He nodded. "You've been right all along."

"I have?"

He nodded once more. "I'm here working for…another interested party. A party whose specific interests lie in your father's pharmaceutical company. A party who wants your father's pharmaceutical company to further his own business, a business that's not exactly sanctioned or condoned by any federal or local law enforcement agencies. You know what I'm sayin' here?"

"Come again?" she asked.

"I'm here working for the mob, Angel. And we want Ellison Pharmaceuticals to further our drug trade."

She gaped at him. *"What?"*

He arched his brows philosophically and nodded at her. "Yeah, everything you've suspected about me and my motives has been right on the mark."

"It has?"

He chuckled at her expression. "Don't look so surprised, Angel. Have a little more faith in yourself as a journalist. I don't know how you did it, but your investigations panned out. Face it. You did a good job."

She smiled a little nervously, clearly torn now between being wary of him and proud of herself. "Thanks," she said a little tentatively. "I knew I was right. I knew you were a lowlife, scumbag, murdering—"

"A little *too* good a job," he interrupted her again, dropping his voice to a dangerous pitch. "If you know what I mean."

She stared at him in silence for a moment, and he was fascinated to observe the obvious workings of her brain, however slow the mechanism seemed to be at the moment. "I'm not sure I *do* know what you mean," she said finally.

He took a leisurely step toward her. "Oh, sure you do. Try harder."

She narrowed her eyes at him. "Nope. Sorry. I'm still coming up blank."

Another lazy step forward brought him a bit nearer to her. "You've gotten a little too close to what's going on in Endicott," he told her, hoping he was dosing her with just the right amount of mystery and suspense. "You've made a few people a little…anxious."

"What, um, wh-what kind of people?" she stammered.

Instead of answering her, he simply grinned and added, "And they've asked me to…do something about you."

She swallowed visibly. "Do something about me?"

He nodded silently as he stepped forward once more.

"Like…like what?" she asked.

He shrugged noncommittally as he took another step. "Like get you out of the picture."

"Out…out of the picture?"

Another step toward her. "Like put you on ice."

"P-put me on ice?"

One more step toward her. "Like…off you."

"O-o-o-off me?" She gaped at him. "You said mobsters didn't say things like that."

"They don't," he concurred. "I was just trying to put what they want me to do to you in polite terms that you could understand."

She swallowed again, and said nothing.

"But I told them I had a better idea where you're concerned." He took one final step to close what small gap remained between them. "What with you having admired me from afar and all that. What with those two little…passionate interludes we had. What with you wanting me to tie you up and all."

"But—"

"So, Angel, here's the deal," he continued without letting

her comment. "You and me are going to get married, A-S-A-P. And then you're going to stop insinuating the things you've been insinuating in print. You don't want to sully the good name of your husband. It will be your name, too, after all, once we tie the knot." He smiled devilishly. "No pun intended."

"Oh, no, I don't think—"

"Unless you're one of those modern women who want to keep their names after they get married, in which case, we need to have a little chat, because I'm kind of old-fashioned that way myself."

"No, I meant I don't think—"

"And this marriage is a good idea, too, because if things *do* happen to get a little…uncomfortable—with the law enforcement folks, I mean—then you won't be able to testify against your darling husband in a court of law."

"No, no, you don't under—"

"It took a lot of doing, but I managed to convince the big boys that you're really crazy in love with me, that your articles in the paper were just your way of getting back at me because I dallied with another woman."

"Whoa, whoa, whoa, this is getting really bizarre, and—"

"But now I've seen the error of my ways and decided I am in fact a gentleman who prefers blondes, so I'm going to give in to all your begging and pleading and make an honest woman out of you."

"Oh, well, thank you *so* much for that measly considera—"

"And that, finally, Angel, oughta shut you up once and for all."

Any fear she might have had for her safety had obviously fled by the time he concluded his offer, to be replaced with indignation at his manner of proposal.

"Shut me up?" she asked, her voice so soft, so level, so calm, he knew she was about to explode. "Shut me up?"

"Either marry me," he said, "or face the consequences. Those consequences being that you kind of disappear. Indefinitely. You know what I'm saying?"

She expelled a breath of air that was almost a chuckle. "Gee, what a choice. Well, here's a news flash for you, Mr. Zorn. I'm a journalist. I won't be shut up. Not by you, not by your threats, not by anybody."

"Is that so?"

She nodded firmly. "Yeah. That's so."

"I was afraid you might say that."

They stared at each other in silence for some moments, each daring the other to back down, neither complying with the other's demand. Angie felt herself growing more and more uncomfortable with every tick of the mantel clock, but what was she supposed to do? Life in Endicott hadn't exactly prepared her for the possibility of a mobster breaking into her house and proposing marriage to her. And good manners aside, she just wasn't quite sure what her response should be.

Then, totally unbidden, she felt an odd little sound bubble up from inside her, the sound of her nervousness and anxiety making itself known. And when she saw the look on Ethan's face, she knew that he knew what that sound meant, too. Because his smile turned absolutely predatory. He met her gaze levelly and began to finger the silk necktie dangling from his collar, his expression indicating he had some real serious plans for the accessory.

"What are you going to do?" she heard herself ask, uncertain when she had chosen to speak. "*Now* are you going to tie me up?"

Idiot, idiot, idiot, she chastised herself for a second time, squeezing her eyes shut in both disbelief and embarrassment. What on earth was the matter with her to even bring that up again? She heard Ethan chuckle and snapped her eyes open to find him grinning at her like a cat with a Christmas sardine.

"Well, I guess if you want it that bad, Angel," he told her in that maddeningly smooth voice, "then I'm just gonna have to accommodate you, aren't I?"

That anxious little titter erupted from inside her again, followed by a nervous smile she was unable to control. Ethan continued to meet her gaze, one eyebrow arched in speculation, his fingers still stroking the length of silk as if he couldn't wait to put it to use.

"You're joking, right?" she managed to ask.

His only response was to reach for the knot in his necktie and slowly begin to loosen it.

"You wouldn't dare."

Without a word, he unlooped the perfect Windsor knot at his throat, then began to slowly pull the length of silk free of his collar, inch by leisurely inch.

"Oh, no," she said, extending a hand, palm up, in a gesture to stop him. "Uh-uh. No way."

"Uh-huh," he told her. "Yes way."

"You wouldn't dare," she repeated.

He looped one end of his tie around one fist, then began to curl the other end around his other fist. Giving the length of silk a good, hard tug, he smiled again.

"Ooo, that was a double dare," he said. "And you know what? I never could resist one of those."

Seven

"Look, Angel, if you'd just be reasonable about this, we wouldn't have a problem here."

Angie eyed Ethan Zorn venomously and struggled against the silk necktie that bound her wrists behind one of her kitchen chairs. When she failed to even loosen her bonds, she tried wrestling her ankles free of the silk sash of her own bathrobe, which tied each ankle to a chair leg. Again with no success.

Ethan had discovered the latter item after a thorough search of the apartment to locate some suitable bondage material. He'd been disappointed, upon upending her lingerie drawer, to discover that she preferred knee socks over silk hosiery, but he'd been delighted by the little scrap of pale-gold nothing that he'd stumbled upon hanging on the back of the bathroom door.

He had tied her up nearly a half hour ago, and now sat scarcely a foot in front of her, straddling backward a chair identical to hers—minus the silk bonds, of course—gazing at her in idle speculation.

"*Me* be reasonable?" she said through gritted teeth. "I'm the one tied to a chair, for crying out loud."

He settled his chin on the arm he had draped over the back of the chair and smiled at her. "Well, Angel, you *did* seem to expect it, after all, and I didn't want to disappoint you."

She envisioned circling his throat with her fingers and throttling the life out of him, even flexed her hands ineffectually against her bonds in an effort to make her fantasy a reality. But all she said was, "You're the one who's not being reasonable here. Untie me. Now."

"I think I've been perfectly reasonable," he countered calmly, ignoring her demand. He leaned back and added, "You're just not looking at the big picture here."

Angie gaped at him. "The big picture?" she asked. "The big picture is that some low-life, scumbag, murdering slug has me tied up in my apartment. What's there for me to be unreasonable about?"

He shook his head and made a face of disgust. "You know, I'm getting awfully tired of you calling me a low-life, scumbag, murdering slug. I'll have you know I have *never* murdered anyone." He threw her a meaningful look. "Not yet, anyway."

"Oh, right. Like I'm supposed to believe *that.*"

"It's true," he told her, and if she hadn't known better, she would have sworn he actually sounded hurt that she could suspect him of such a thing. "I'm a *front* man, not a *hit* man," he clarified for her. "Murder isn't in my job description."

She rolled her eyes. Mobsters had job descriptions? What next? Would they be forming a union? Mobsters Local 369. She could just imagine the dues.

"Will you please untie me?" she asked again, wriggling ineffectually at her bonds. "My arms are starting to cramp up."

He looked dashed at that, seeming genuinely concerned that she was uncomfortable. "Well, why didn't you say so?" he asked her. "I can do something about that."

He stood and moved behind her chair, but instead of untying

her wrists, he pressed his palms gently over her forearms. "Where does it hurt?" he asked softly. He stroked his fingers carefully along her lower arm, kneading her muscles gently. "Here?"

The soft brush of his fingertips against her skin affected Angie in a way she wished like crazy she could deny. His touch should make her flesh crawl, she told herself. Not hum happily in desire for more.

But as much as she wished she could hate Ethan Zorn, as much as she wanted to be repulsed by him, she realized she simply could not. In spite of his contemptible occupation, regardless of the way his job forced him to ignore legal and social precedents, despite the fact that he was almost certainly unethical and hopelessly amoral...

She sighed inwardly. He seemed like such a nice guy. He was funny, he was smart, he was gorgeous, he was sexy. He was even gentle, tender and caring in an odd sort of way. And Angie was helpless not to respond to him as she would any man who shared those traits.

He's an admitted criminal, she reminded herself. *He told you flat out he's here working for the mob, and he wants to take your father's company for criminal purposes, for God's sake.*

Yeah, but he was *so cute,* she reminded herself right back. And besides, her response to him wasn't entirely her fault. Bob had a hand in it, too, didn't he? Under normal circumstances, she *would* be repulsed by Ethan Zorn, wouldn't she? It was just that Bob had everyone in Endicott acting strangely. Didn't he? Angie couldn't help it if she was attracted to a criminal. Could she? That was all Bob's doing, right?

Right?

"Does this help at all?" she heard Ethan ask, his voice sounding rough and uneven and very, very close.

As he pressed his fingers firmly but gently into her achy muscles, she could feel his warm breath dancing in her hair, and the scent of him—something clean and conservative and utterly at odds with the kind of man he was—surrounded her.

As she felt his touch creep confidently along her arms from wrist to elbow, Angie's blood suddenly began to race through her body, spreading heat and a strange kind of tingling sensation through her entire system. Her heart began to pound ferociously, and her breathing came in restive, shallow little gasps she hoped he couldn't hear.

"A…a…a little higher," she managed to say. "Just above my elbows."

She couldn't see him—she could only feel his presence behind her, and the light skim of his fingertips tripping along her arm. Somehow the denial of the sight of him heartened her. In not being able to see him, she could pretend that the man whose touch was sending her entire system into overdrive was someone else, someone more suitable, the kind of man it would be okay for her to fall in love with.

As he dragged his fingers up her arm and over her elbow, Angie closed her eyes and tried to envision such a man in place of Ethan Zorn. A good man, a decent man, a man she would be proud to call her own. But the vision that took root in her mind's eye was of a black-haired man with beatific brown eyes, eyes that countered every bad thing that existed in the world. The good man who came to Angie in her reverie, the decent one to supersede the bad one, was none other than Ethan Zorn.

She couldn't imagine why her brain would betray her in such a way, didn't know why reason—what little she normally cultivated, anyway—had fled. Bob had a hand in it, naturally, she told herself again, but even at that…

There was just something about Ethan that wasn't quite right, something about the man that was at odds with his profession. She didn't know how she could be so certain of that, but somehow, Angie knew—she *knew*—he wasn't what he was claiming to be. Not only was he *not* a sales rep for the Cokely Chemical Corporation, but he wasn't a mobster, either.

Or, at the very least, he wasn't a bad man at heart.

She wished she had time to try to figure him out, even started to make some quick diagnoses of everything that had led up to her assumptions about him in the first place, in the hope that she might trip over something she'd missed the first time around. But he chose that moment to skim his fingers a bit higher—up over her shoulders and around her neck—and Angie's thought processes dried up entirely.

"Oh," she murmured when he grazed his thumb along her jaw. "Oh, Ethan…"

It was the first time she had called him by his first name, and the designation felt strangely familiar rolling off her tongue. She felt him move closer behind her, felt him bend until his head was level with hers.

"Does that make you feel better?" he asked, his voice low and sweet.

She nodded slowly. "Oh, yes."

"So your arms don't hurt anymore?"

This time she shook her head slowly. "No. I feel really, um, really, uh…good. *Really* good."

She heard him chuckle softly. "I'm glad. Suddenly, I don't feel so bad myself."

She wanted to say more, even opened her mouth to do so, but the words shriveled up in her throat. Ethan had moved his head closer to hers, until his rough jaw brushed easily against her downy one. The touch of his fingers skimming along the line of her jaw and her nape created a soft, scintillating friction that shook her to her core. She heard his breathing become thready and uneven, echoing her own erratic respiration. Angie kept her eyes closed and allowed herself to enjoy the sensation for a moment, reveling in the closeness of him, the scent of him, the feel of him.

And suddenly, she found herself wanting to touch him, too. She wanted to brush the backs of her hands along his warm flesh, wanted to score his hair with her fingers, wanted to press her palms along the ridges of muscle that she somehow knew corded his back and chest. As if acting of their own will, her fingers flexed, and her wrists strained at the necktie still containing them. It was no fair, she thought. She was bound to a chair, unable to follow her instincts and desires, while Ethan had free rein to do whatever he wanted to...

Ethan.

"Yes, Angel?"

Only then did she realize she had uttered his name out loud, and in the kind of voice a woman only used when she wanted a man to carry her to sensual, sexual heights she'd never visited before. She knew that, because he had responded in the kind of voice men only used when they wanted to do just that to a woman.

Get a grip, Angie, she commanded herself silently. *The man may be sexy, but he's also probably wanted in a dozen states.*

Ooo, I'll say he's wanted, she answered herself immediately. *Especially in Indiana.*

Angie squeezed her eyes shut tight and did everything she possibly could to squelch her body's traitorous reaction to Ethan Zorn. She thought about icy cold rivers. She recalled the smell of sauerkraut. She remembered how she used to find her brother's pet chameleon in her shoes the hard way. She thought about Ernest Borgnine as a romantic lead. She reminded herself how the IRS really stuck it to single people.

To absolutely no avail.

In spite of her best efforts to kill off the arousal he had sparked in her, the soft touch of Ethan's fingers idling along her jaw and neck kept creeping into her brain, into her psyche, into her libido. And Angie, God help her, felt herself falling deeper and deeper, and more completely under his spell.

"Ethan..." she said again.

"Hmm?"

Not good, she thought. Not good at all. He sounded even more aroused than she did. "That isn't, um...that's not, uh...not going to work," she told him, hoping she wasn't about to make a liar out of herself.

For a moment, he didn't reply, but simply continued his gentle foray, stroking the pad of his thumb along the column of her throat, brushing his fingertips along the line of her jaw. Finally, he asked quietly, "What's not going to work?"

''That, um, that thing you're doing with your hands.''

His thumb dipped lower, tracing the line of her collarbone beneath her shirt. She managed to swallow a soft sound of surrender, but was helpless to prevent the wistful sigh that curled up from some dark, lonely place deep inside her.

''What thing I'm doing with my hands?'' he asked as his other hand moved to the other side of her collarbone, repeating the same languid, easy caresses. Back and forth, from the hollow at the base of her throat out to her shoulders and back again, he skimmed his rough fingertips along her warm skin.

''That thing,'' she said a little breathlessly, scarcely knowing now why she had objected to his touch in the first place.

''What, that thing?'' he asked, brushing his thumb slowly along the length of her collarbone and back once again. ''Or *that* thing?'' he added, dragging his index finger down to her first button, toying alternately with it and with the warm flesh beneath.

Angie's breath caught in her throat, but she managed a strangled, ''Both things. They're not going to work. You're not going to change my mind. You're not going to intimidate me into marrying you.''

His hands paused, one hovering over her button, the other curling back around her nape to tangle gently in the hair. She shivered at the sharp, sweet sensation that spiraled through her, trying to quell the tiny bursts of heat that exploded everywhere he touched her. But her body, her traitorous, fickle body, in spite of its bonds, moved toward Ethan's heat the way a comet is drawn to the sun. He was magnetic, compelling. And she simply could not resist him.

''At this point, Angel,'' he said, his voice sounding as strangled as her own, ''I've pretty much given up trying to intimidate you.''

''You...you have?'' she murmured, marveling at the depth of her disappointment.

He paused only long enough to bury his fingers more thoroughly in her hair and push his hand more completely into her shirt. Angie sucked in a quick little breath at the invasion, and unwittingly arched her back more fully into his touch.

"Yeah," he said as his fingers encountered the wisp of lace that covered her breast. "At this point, I've decided to try seducing you, instead. It would make the marriage a lot more interesting, don't you think?"

Her heart halted for a nanosecond, then began beating fast enough to make her dizzy. "You're not going to do that, either," she assured him in a less-than-certain voice. "I won't be seduced by a...by a..."

"By a low-life, scumbag, murdering slug?" His voice was flat, emotionless, and his fingers stilled completely.

"Right," she said, the word scarcely a whisper.

He began to skim his hands gingerly over her warm skin once more. "Gee, then I guess I'll just have to prove to you that I'm not that kind of man, won't I?"

As much as she hated to make the assertion, she told him, "You'll never convince me of that."

"Oh?" he countered, his voice now low and dangerous. "Just watch me."

Slowly, so slowly that Angie could have voiced a protest if she'd tried, Ethan pushed his hand lower until it covered her breast. Then he palmed her lightly, pressing his open fingers over the lower curve of her breast, lifting, squeezing, possessing. She bit back a moan and tried to stanch the ripple of delight that echoed through her. With no success at all.

Her silence must have encouraged him, because he released her and moved his hand higher, then quickly dipped his fingers beneath the soft lace that was the last barrier between her flesh and his. As quietly as a whisper, he urged his hand lower, until he cradled her breast fully in the warmth of his palm.

As one, they expelled soft sighs of completion, Angie arching her back hungrily toward his caress, Ethan closing his fingers more resolutely over her.

"Your skin is so soft, Angel," he whispered near her ear. "So hot. You running a fever I should know about?"

"Please," she murmured, not certain whether she was objecting to something or pleading for something, only knowing she had to make some effort to slow his progress before she lost herself to him irrevocably.

"Please what?" he asked as he continued to cup her lazily, squeezing her warm flesh gently. The pad of his index finger found the ripe center of her breast, and Angie gasped as he drew an idle circle over the stiff flesh.

"Please..." she said again, still not sure what she wanted him to do. Reason seemed to have left her, to be replaced by a raging, riotous need that superseded everything she knew to be right and true. She clenched her hands into fists and struggled against her bonds again, but instead of a desire to be free of him, she found herself wanting to throw herself into his arena forever.

"Please what?" he asked again, his voice softer and more ragged than hers was.

He curled his hand completely over the warm curve of her breast, silently stating his possession of her. An explosion of heat and sensation rocked her, and Angie squirmed in her chair in a fruitless effort to free herself. Once more, she tried to liberate her hands from behind herself, and once more, she found herself completely restrained. The recognition of that fact finally jelled in her brain, and when she remembered that he had bound her, she finally found the impetus to halt the progress of whatever was happening to the two of them.

"Please stop it," she whispered, her tone of voice nowhere near as insistent as she'd hoped to make it.

In spite of that, Ethan stilled behind her, and the hand on her breast, with one final, gentle squeeze, relaxed. Angie held her breath as he slowly—oh, God, so slowly—dragged his hand from inside her shirt, loosed the hair he had wound in his fist and took a step backward. Only when he strode around the chair to stand in front of her did she open her eyes and inhale breath again, however unsteadily.

He dropped down onto his haunches and looked up at her, pinning her with a gaze that was at once solicitous and demanding. "There's something between us, Angel," he told her, "something very, very strong. Blame it on Bob if you want to, but I think it's something that's a lot faster and a lot more elemental than a burning hunk of rock hurtling through space."

Angie knew that to contradict him would be lying, and she knew he knew that, too. So she simply remained silent, meeting his gaze as levelly as she could, trying to breathe as evenly as possible to slow her wild pulse rate.

"But I promise you," he added, "that I won't touch you again unless—until—you ask me to. Even after we get married."

"We're not getting married," she told him, the words sounding too quiet, too uncertain. "And you're not touching me again."

"Not until you ask me to," he repeated.

"Then it won't happen."

"We'll see."

He reached down and began to untie the knots at her ankles, and when he'd freed her legs, moved silently behind her to work free the necktie that bound her wrists. Angie immediately brought her arms forward, wincing a bit at the brief, sharp pain that shot through her.

"I'm sorry," Ethan told her, seeming genuinely regretful for what he had done. He wound up his necktie and stuffed it into his jacket pocket. "I just wanted you to listen to reason, and I couldn't think of any other way to make you do that."

She expelled an incredulous little chuckle. "Maybe you should try talking to me reasonably."

His eyebrows shot up in surprise, as if he honestly hadn't considered that course of action. "Okay. You want reasonable, you got it."

He returned to his earlier position, straddling the chair opposite her. For a long moment, he said nothing, only watched her as if he were replaying in his mind every touch, every sound, every nuance of what had just transpired between the two of them. His expression became dreamy and distant, and a soft smile curled his features.

Angie began to fear that he would never speak again, so she cleared her throat a little roughly in an effort to bring him back around. It took a few more minutes of him staring vacantly out into space, but he finally seemed to regain his focus, and fixed his gaze on hers.

"Here's the way it is, Angel," he began, his voice still sounding a little faraway, his eyes still soft and uncertain. "You've been nosin' around in places where you shouldn't have, and now you've got a lot of people scared that you're gonna expose them."

Angie tried to keep up with the sudden change in subject matter and mood, but her head was still spinning from the electrically charged exchange the two of them had just shared. In spite of that, she managed to tell him, "That's because I *am* going to expose them. Eventually."

"You do that," he told her, "and you're gonna wind up getting hurt."

He wasn't threatening her this time, she realized. Nor was he even warning her. What Ethan was doing now, she could see, was simply stating a fact. If she continued to delve into her investigation, someone was going to come after her. That's all there was to it. And strangely enough, that seemed to bother him as much as it bothered her.

"Okay," she said reluctantly. "Then I'll back off."

"Not good enough."

"What do you mean it's not good enough?" she demanded, riled now because she was giving him what he wanted, and it still wasn't enough.

"It's too little, too late," he told her. "You don't understand. These are big, tough guys who flout the law for a living. And you've scared them."

He stood up quickly enough to send his chair toppling forward, then moved to stoop before her again. Somehow, he seemed to be supplicating himself, and however ridiculous, that heartened her some.

"You've scared them," he repeated emphatically. "And

they don't like to be scared, Angel. Especially by some little small-town female.''

She gaped at him and swallowed hard. ''Oh, well,'' she said softly, ''excuse the hell outta me.''

''They want you out of the picture,'' he continued as if she hadn't spoken. ''They want you to disappear. You know what I'm sayin' here?''

Angie swallowed anxiously again, her bravado failing her now. She wanted to toss off something flip and unconcerned to counter him, but for the life of her, she could think of nothing to say.

''Why do you care what happens to me?'' she asked him. ''You yourself said I've been a pain in the butt. Seems like you might not mind having me disappear.''

His eyebrows arrowed down at her assertion, and he lifted his hand to cup her cheek gently in his palm. ''I care,'' he said softly. ''I don't wanna see you get hurt.''

She really couldn't think of anything to say in response to that, so she only met his gaze levelly in silence. He stroked the pad of his thumb once over her cheek, then dropped his hand back to his side.

''The thing is,'' he went on as if the odd little exchange had never happened, ''they might feel different if they had you on their side. Where they can keep an eye on you at all times.'' He hesitated a moment, then added, ''Where *I* can keep an eye on you at all times.''

''But—''

''Look, you don't really have to marry me,'' he told her. ''We just have to make the big boys think you did.''

She eyed him curiously. ''What do you mean?''

''I mean we just have to pretend to get married. I think that would be enough, for now, to at least keep my superiors and colleagues at a distance. And it would give me a reason for being around you all the time, night and day, that wouldn't raise eyebrows and sully your good reputation in town.''

''What happens after 'for now'?'' she asked, amazed to discover that she was actually considering his proposal, however phony the arrangement would be. It was unthinkable, she told herself. It was stupid. It was unnecessary.

But, gee, what if he was right? What if she really was in danger? What if being perceived as his wife was something that would keep that danger at a minimum?

"By that time," Ethan continued, oblivious to the incoherent babbling her brain had undertaken with itself, "my business here should be concluded."

"I thought you were going to take my father's company," she reminded him. "Wouldn't that sort of keep you guys—or a reasonable facsimile thereof—in Endicott on a permanent basis? In which case," she rushed on, "I'd have to go back to crusading against you."

"I didn't say we're definitely taking your father's company. I said we're just looking at it."

"What if you do take it?" she insisted.

He inhaled an impatient breath and released it as a groan of frustration. "Angel, will you just trust me?"

She widened her eyes at the question. "Trust you? *Trust you?* Are you serious?"

He nodded. "Yeah, I am."

Angie studied Ethan long and hard and wondered if she could possibly trust her instincts when a rogue comet was out there in the stratosphere making people do and say the damnedest things. Because her instincts told her that she actually *should* trust Ethan Zorn. Her instincts were clear in their belief that he honestly feared for her safety and cared deeply about what happened to her. Her instincts were insistent that he was a good guy, looking out for her welfare.

But just how far could she trust her instincts? she asked herself again.

Ethan seemed to take her silence as a good sign, because he continued, "I've got a friend in Philly who used to be a man of the cloth. Unfortunately, he couldn't keep his hands out of the collection plate—he had a bookie to support—and his license to...to..." He sighed and extended his hand forward, as if he were physically reaching for the right word.

"To…be reverend," he finally finished, "was revoked. So he left the church and now he works for us."

"A former man of the cloth is now working for the mob," Angie reiterated, in case she hadn't heard right.

Ethan lifted a shoulder negligently, then let it drop. "Hey, we need spiritual guidance as much as the next guy."

"Yeah, I'll say."

He let that slide and went on, "Anyway, I've already talked to him, and he said he can arrange everything. He'll make it look like you're marrying me, without you actually having to take the plunge. So to speak."

Meaning, Angie assumed, either pretend to take the marital plunge with Ethan, or take a much less figurative one into a river, wrapped in a tarp.

"It's a crazy idea, Ethan," she said, wondering why she was suddenly so comfortable with calling him by his first name.

"You don't have much choice, Angel."

"Maybe I could print a retraction in the paper."

He shook his head. "Not good enough."

She thought harder. "Maybe I could just leave town for a little while."

"They'll find you."

"Not if I—"

"They'll find you," he repeated, his eyes dark and altogether too serious for her comfort.

She met his gaze steadily, but remained silent, trying to come up with something—anything—that would make for a better alternative. But not a single idea entered her brain that seemed more effective than the sham marriage Ethan was proposing.

Would it really be so awful? she asked herself. It would only be temporary. And the two of them did get along in a bizarre kind of way. As much as she hated to admit it, she sort of liked Ethan. Maybe more than a nice, normal, sane woman should, but still…

He'd promised not to touch her again. Not unless she asked

for it, which of course she wouldn't. Not in a million zillion years. Not even with Bob hanging on the horizon. But could she really trust someone who broke the law for a living? Then again, what choice did she have if other criminals were looking to...to...to off her?

"So, Angel," she heard Ethan say through the hazy fog of questions that kept circling in her brain. "I need to know. You gonna marry me, or what?"

Eight

"**I** now pronounce you husband and wife."

Angie heard the announcement through a haze of fog and asked herself yet again how Ethan Zorn had managed to talk her into such a crazy scheme, and what on earth she thought she was doing, marrying the guy.

Saving your buttinsky neck, that's what, she told herself immediately. *Doing what you have to do to keep the mob from putting you on ice.*

How, oh, how, had she gotten herself mixed up in such a mess? she wondered. Oh, yeah. Now she remembered. Fifteen years ago she had wished upon a comet—she had asked for something exciting to happen in her hometown. And Bob, God love him, had brought her Ethan Zorn. How nice of Bob. How thoughtful. That damned comet had even arranged for Angie's wedding—however superficially—and now she was married to the mob. She supposed she wasn't likely to find much more excitement than that. Not in Endicott, anyway.

So often, when she'd been a girl, she had fantasized about

what her wedding day would be like. She had dressed her Barbie in the white lace wedding gown her aunt Emma had made by hand, then she'd filched her brother's G.I. Joe and dressed him in his formal U.S. Marines uniform, complete with sword. She'd walked the two dolls down the upstairs hallway—also known as Westminster Abbey—and there, with Barbie's best friend Christie acting as archbishop, Angie had played out the most beautiful wedding scene the world had ever known.

Of course, that particular wedding scene had been in no way similar to the one in which Angie had just copped a starring role as bride. Instead of a beautiful, handmade, white lace gown that flowed into eternity, she'd been forced to hurriedly buy off the rack at Hildy's Bridal. And there had been only one dress in her size left in stock, now that bridal's high season was over—a skintight, ivory satin sheath, with a bow-shaped bustle the size of Argentina and a neckline cut down to Tierra del Fuego. The headpiece was even more surreal, a spangled, beaded creation more suited to a Vegas show hall than a small-town chapel.

Ethan, on the other hand, looked cool and calm, dark and dangerous, and completely comfortable in the role of groom. His black tuxedo was understated and elegant, undecorated save the pink rosebud pinned to his lapel. He'd forgone the traditional butterfly collar and bow tie, in favor of a collarless white shirt fastened at the neck with a single, solid gold stud. Angie had to stifle a sigh every time she looked at him, so handsome, so sexy, did he appear.

At least some small part of her girlhood fantasy had played out the right way, she tried to reassure herself. Even better than her dreams, actually. G.I. Joe in his dress blues had nothing on Ethan Zorn in evening black.

"You may now kiss the bride."

The announcement brought Angie up short, jerking her out of her ruminations with the force of a Mack truck. She'd forgotten all about the public kiss to seal their union. But clearly, Ethan hadn't.

Before she could say a word, he swept her into his arms and covered her mouth with his, plying her lips with the intensity and dexterity of a man who was stamping his own personal seal of approval on the union that had just occurred. He pulled away long enough for her to catch her breath, then kissed her a second time, with even more gusto. Hoots of support and catcalls of delight erupted from the groom's side of the room, while a few nervous titters and uncertain applause rose from the bride's.

When Ethan finally released her, Angie stumbled backward, nearly tumbling down the altar steps. He laughed and reached out to steady her, then scooped her into his arms. As the organ exploded into a merry rendition of the theme song to *The Newlywed Game,* Ethan laughed and carried her back down the aisle to the accompaniment of now wild applause.

And all the way back, all she could do was stare at him dumbfounded. He was going to be viewed by everyone in town as her husband now. Her husband. Her *husband.* And one thought kept circling and circling in Angie's head above all others.

Tonight—for all intents and purposes, in the scheme of things as they stood now—was her wedding night.

To complete the charade of their sham marriage, Ethan had reserved the honeymoon suite for them at the Admiralty Inn, Endicott's answer to the Four Seasons Hotel—or rather, Endicott's answer to a really good Quality Inn; there was no answer to the Four Seasons in Endicott. Yet in spite of his vow not to touch her again—unless of course, she asked him to, which, naturally, she would not—Angie couldn't help but wonder just how much farther than the rental of a hotel room Ethan was planning to take the charade.

More important than that, though, she asked herself, just how far was *she* planning to take it? After the way she'd succumbed to his proposal a week ago, not to mention how quickly and easily she'd melted into him those times when he'd kissed her, she honestly wasn't sure.

She supposed that was all up to Bob. This was, after all,

the weekend when the comet would be making his closest pass to the planet, peak time for odd behavior from the local citizenry. Angie told herself if she could just hold on for a few more days, then Bob's effects would begin to wane, and she could go back to being her old self again. That old self being a woman who found men like Ethan contemptible and in no way arousing.

Just a few days, she told herself. Surely she could resist him for that length of time.

When the couple passed through the doors of the sanctuary and into the vestibule, Ethan stopped and settled Angie back on her feet. It took her a moment to find her balance, but even after she did, he kept one arm looped around her waist. She glanced up to find him smiling down at her, and her heart hammered in her chest.

He looked so happy, she marveled. He looked as though he was genuinely pleased by what had just happened. She didn't understand how that could be. Surely this was going to put just as big a crimp in his lifestyle as it would hers. How was he supposed to go about being a low-life, scumbag, murdering slug if he had to worry about the old ball and chain nagging him for his paycheck when he came home from work every night?

But before Angie could say a word, they were suddenly surrounded by well-wishers, and she had to shift gears again into faux-bride mode. She had to pretend to be as happy as Ethan was pretending to be, and oddly enough, for some reason, that wasn't such a stretch at all.

By the time they reached the Elks' Lodge for the reception, Angie's jaw was beginning to ache from smiling for all the photographs. Again, she'd had to fake her delirious delight at her newfound marital status, and again, she'd discovered an ease and comfort with the sham that surprised her. At one point, when the photographer was restaging the kiss to seal the union, Angie found herself actually believing that what she was experiencing was indeed the happiest day of her life.

Certainly, she consoled herself, it was the most exciting.

However, once the newlyweds reached the reception hall, and once she got another good look at the groom's side of the festivities, she remembered exactly what kind of man she had attached herself to. Absorbing the guests who had traveled to Endicott from Philadelphia to celebrate the nuptials of their native son and co-worker, Angie had to shake her head in disbelief.

What a motley bunch they were. She suddenly found herself wishing she owned stock in Brylcreem and Aqua Velva. She could have made a killing as long as Ethan's cohorts were around.

Then she grimaced at her wording. Doubtless it would be Ethan's cohorts who made any killings around Endicott. Or at least they would have been, had she not married into the mob and become one of their own.

Angie swallowed with some difficulty and followed Ethan to the head of the receiving line. "What did you say that one guy's name is?" she asked. She pointed discreetly at a short, round man standing beside a woman who wore a hat with enough birds affixed to it to qualify for a prop in a Hitchcock movie. "Goosey Lucy?"

Ethan followed the direction she indicated, but seemed distracted as he replied, "Something like that."

"What kind of a name is 'Goosey Lucy'?" she asked further. "And those other guys you introduced me to... No-Brains Mankowicz. And Slant-Nose Eddie. And Lenny... Lenny...what was his last name again?"

"Bagagroceries," Ethan answered shortly.

"That's it," Angie recalled. "Lenny Bagagroceries. Oh, and let's not forget Lenny's lovely wife, Hotsie Bagagroceries. Ethan," she complained, tugging hard on his arm.

"What?"

She eyed him pleadingly. "How am I supposed to introduce your friends to my parents? None of them have normal names."

He frowned at her. "Oh, that's something coming from a

woman who claims among her own acquaintances people with names like Boomer and Tippy.''

She narrowed her eyes at him in warning.

He sighed heavily. ''Come on, Angel, I want you to meet someone.''

''Who?''

''My boss.''

That shut her up. The last person Angie wanted to meet was Mr. Big. What was the protocol when one was dealing with crime bosses? she wondered. Was she supposed to drop to her knees and kiss his ring? Ask him if he would be needing any horses' heads while he was in town? Would he mind if she called him ''Don''?

''Ethan, I don't think it's a good idea,'' she said as she tripped along behind him, trying to slow their progress.

''Why not?'' he asked. ''He wants to meet you.''

''Well, there is that small matter of him initially wanting me dead,'' she reminded him.

Ethan halted in his tracks. ''Oh, yeah. I forgot about that.''

She gaped at him. ''You forgot? You forgot that the man in charge wanted to put your wife on ice?''

He shrugged. ''Well, you weren't my wife at the time.''

She shook her head at him. ''Let's start the food line. Everyone's got to be hungry.''

But when Angie spun around to do just that, she found herself face to face with her two best friends in the world, and they were glaring at her with disappointment. Rosemary and Kirby had made no secret of their suspicion—nor of their fear for her safety—where Angie's sudden engagement and very quick wedding were concerned. And now, even after the fact, they still looked pretty steamed and plenty concerned. Ethan seemed to notice that, too, because he quickly excused himself to go greet his employer on his own.

''There's still time to get out of this,'' Rosemary said without preamble once Ethan's departure placed him clearly out of earshot. ''Kirby and I can shelter you. That low-life, scumbag, murdering slug will never find you.''

"He'd find me," Angie replied wearily. "Or worse, his 'associates' would find me. Those guys have ways."

"There's someone who might be able to help," Kirby assured her. The concern in her voice outweighed the look of sadness in her eyes. "James has a lot of money, and he owns property all over the world. Maybe I could call him and—"

"Oh, so it's *'James'* now, is it?" Angie interrupted her friend. "What happened to 'that promiscuous, playboy, Peeping Tom,' hmm?"

Kirby had the decency to look embarrassed as she directed her gaze to the floor. "Um, things have sort of changed a little bit," she said softly.

Angie and Rosemary exchanged very interested looks. "In what way?" Angie asked when she returned her attention to Kirby.

Kirby shuffled her feet a little awkwardly. "I, uh…I don't want to talk about it."

Angie opened her mouth to press the issue, but Rosemary prevented her by adding, "Willis thinks you're being dumb about this."

Angie rolled her eyes heavenward. "Willis thinks everyone except himself is dumb, Rosemary, unless you've forgotten. Especially you and your friends."

Rosemary lifted her chin defensively. "He's not like he used to be," she said, surprising Angie. "He's changed. In some respects, anyway."

The last thing Rosemary had ever tried to do was stand up for Willis Random. On the contrary, she had generally been his biggest and most outspoken critic.

"In what respects?" Angie asked, unable to picture Willis as anything other than the pizza-faced little twerp who had taken so much pleasure in taunting Rosemary all through high school.

Rosemary threw a glance back over her shoulder. "See for yourself. He came to the wedding. As my, um…as my date."

Angie's eyebrows shot up in surprise. "You're dating Willis? Where is he?"

"He's over there talking to the minister and your mom."

Angie craned her neck to look past Rosemary, and saw her mother standing between Ethan's friend/spiritual guide/partner in crime and a drop-dead gorgeous guy who bore absolutely no resemblance to her memory of Willis Random. The man stood over six feet tall, his broad shoulders straining against his tweed jacket, his horn-rimmed glasses making him look serious and intelligent and oddly sexy in a Clark Kent kind of way…and in no way twerpish.

"That's Willis?" Angie asked incredulously.

Rosemary nodded silently, her gaze following Angie's. And if Angie hadn't known better, she would have sworn her friend was actually pining for the boy-turned-man who had always made her feel so small and insignificant.

"And you guys are still shacking up together at your house?" she asked her friend.

Rosemary nodded again. "My mom decreed it as mayor, after all. I, um…I'd rather not talk about it. And speaking of mothers," she added in a rush, before Angie could press the issue of her cohabitation with her arch enemy, "how does your mother feel about you marrying a criminal?"

Angie sighed heavily. "Are you kidding? My mom and dad are deliriously happy. They think Ethan is just the greatest guy to come down the pike. They don't know he's a criminal. Heck, my dad is already thinking about all the great deals he's going to get, now that he has a son-in-law who works for a chemical company. They think he's transferring to Endicott, that we're going to buy the house up the street from them and start a family right away."

"You told them that?" Rosemary asked with a gasp.

Angie shook her head. "No. Ethan told them that. I could kill him for it, too."

Rosemary and Kirby both shook their heads, their faces reflecting identical expressions of being clearly let down. But before Angie could offer them any further reassurance, she felt a strong hand clamp down on her upper arm. She turned to find Ethan standing behind her, and if she hadn't known better, she would have thought he was using her as a shield to keep her two best friends at bay.

"I think we need to start the food line," he told her. "Some of my...associates...are getting restless. You don't wanna let these guys go too long without eating. Trust me." After a moment's thought, he added, "We are serving some kind of red meat, aren't we?"

Eventually the newlyweds did manage to make their way to the buffet and loaded their plates with shrimp puffs, Vienna sausages and carrot sticks, then found themselves assaulted by well-wishers again. Just as they finally found their seats at the head table and sat down to eat, the hired disc jockey stepped up to the microphone and introduced the newly united couple, inviting them to step up to the dance floor for their first promenade as man and wife.

Ethan dropped the shrimp puff he had lifted to his mouth, smiled at Angie with resignation and extended his hand to her. She forced a watery smile in response, then wove her fingers with his, and together they strode to the middle of the room. With a crackle and a hiss, the speakers blared the opening bars for "The Eyes of a Woman in Love" from *Guys and Dolls*. As the DJ adjusted the volume, Angie bit back a laugh and tried not to feel so good.

"Who chose this song?" she asked as Ethan folded his arms over her back and pulled her close.

He grinned down at her, and again she experienced the odd sensation that he was genuinely pleased by this marital turn of events, however phony they were. "I did," he told her. "It just seemed appropriate somehow."

"Mmm-hmm," she murmured noncommittally, nestling her head against his chest. After a moment of silent swaying to and fro, she added, "I love this song. That's one of my favorite movies."

She sensed his hesitation, then heard him inquire softly, "Yeah, but is the song appropriate?"

"I could ask you the same question," she replied, still not

looking at him. "Part of the lyrics talk about the eyes of a man who's in love, too, you know."

"Yeah, I know."

"So?"

"So what?"

She moved her body eloquently in time with his, but continued to keep her gaze fixed on the crowd surrounding them. "So is the song appropriate?"

For a moment, she thought he wouldn't answer, then he responded so quietly she almost didn't hear him. "I asked you first."

Something warm and gooey settled in her stomach, but she avoided a reply to his question by suggesting, "Maybe you should have chosen the theme song for the movie *Angel and the Badman,* instead."

For a moment, he didn't reply, and she worried that maybe she had overstepped the bounds. Why she kept worrying about offending a felon, and why she was wondering whether the two of them would even consider the idea of love, she still couldn't understand. She was about to look up at him, about to apologize, when his arms tightened around her a bit.

"But would *that* be appropriate, either?" he asked softly.

A strange little bubble of something she decided she'd rather not contemplate burst in her belly, spreading a heat unlike anything she'd ever experienced before throughout her entire system. Instead of answering Ethan's question, she simply snuggled closer to him, circling his waist with her arms, moving her body up against his.

At the moment, she didn't know what to think. Her rational mind told her this man was indeed bad, someone from whom she should keep her distance at all costs. But her heart told her something else entirely. Ethan Zorn was an enigma, plain and simple. His occupation was one reserved for lowlifes and creeps. But she knew deep down that he was neither of those things.

She didn't know for sure exactly *what* he was, but he wasn't a bad man. Not really. Now, if she could just figure out exactly how to uncover the *real* Ethan Zorn, she could refine her role as Mrs. Zorn.

Mrs. Zorn. The title was so strange. It sounded like it belonged to someone else entirely. Unfortunately, she was going to have to get used to hearing it. At least for a little while. Until she could figure out how to untangle herself and her family from the web of intrigue she'd managed to mix them all up in.

Something exciting. That's what she had wished for fifteen years ago. And boy, had Bob granted her wish. If she had it all to do over again…

Angie closed her eyes and bit back a sigh of contentment that came out of nowhere. Ethan's heart thumped steadily beneath her ear, his arms encircled her with a warmth and concern he couldn't possibly be faking, and if she was honest with herself, she had to admit that she'd never felt more alive, more ebullient, more…happy…than she did at that very moment.

Of course, most of that could be blamed on Bob, she reminded herself, but still… If she had it all to do over again, she told herself…

She would do it exactly the same way.

Why, she couldn't begin to imagine. But somehow she could sense that there was a lot more to Ethan Zorn than he was letting her see. And more than anything else in the world, Angie wanted to find out precisely what—and who—he really was. Lucky for her, she was his wife now. At least, as far as the rest of the world was concerned. And wives had access to their men that other people didn't have. She was just going to need to work a little harder than most women at uncovering her husband's true nature.

But that was okay, she told herself. She was going to be spending lots of time with him, after all. And just because Ethan had allegedly married her didn't mean she was surrendering her quest to discover his real business in Endicott. Oh, maybe she wouldn't be printing her findings in the newspaper, as she'd originally planned—not until it was safe, anyway—

but if he thought he'd thrown her off the track by pretending to marry her, he had another think coming.

So Angie simply smiled a secret little smile to herself and snuggled a bit closer to her new husband. In a matter of hours, they'd be at their hotel, setting off on their wedding night, she reminded herself. And, like any bride on such an occasion, she was sure to uncover all kinds of things about her husband that she'd never even suspected before.

Unfortunately, she thought further as a ripple of apprehension shook her, that would probably entail uncovering all kinds of things about herself she'd never suspected before, either. Not the least of which was just how far she was willing to go to get to the bottom of a riddle named Ethan Zorn that had, of late, been leaving her sleepless at night.

And now that those sleepless nights would involve none other than Ethan himself—and on a much more intimate level at that—she couldn't help but be curious whether warm milk and a good book would be enough to bring her satisfaction.

Tonight, she supposed, she would uncover the answer to that question. That one, and dozens of others, too.

Nine

Ethan studied the brass plaque affixed to the door before him and wondered yet again what the hell he thought he was doing, putting a nice girl like Angie the Angel in the precarious position he'd forced her into. *Honeymoon Suite,* the plaque read in frilly scripted letters that were far too elegant and beautiful to ever be associated with the likes of him.

Honeymoon suite, he repeated to himself. Such a simple, harmless little phrase to be conjuring up such elaborate, troubling images in his mind. Honeymoon suites were things more suited to other people, not him. People who had normal lives that didn't involve strapping on a gun, or roaming the country like a vagabond, or hanging around low-life, scumbag, murdering slugs. People who had something to offer their loved ones other than a life surrounded by crime and danger.

He glanced down at his alleged wife. He had never planned on having one of those, not even on a phony, temporary basis. Not just because he hadn't anticipated ever meeting a woman he could fall in love with in a forever-after kind of way, but because he'd never much thought a woman would fall in love with him—in any way.

A woman still hadn't, he reminded himself. The only reasons Angie was by his side right now were that she feared for her safety and he hadn't given her any other choice. But hey, that was okay, because he didn't love her, either. He couldn't. He wasn't capable of that kind of commitment, or even that kind of emotion.

At least, he amended, gazing down at the elegant profile of the woman he had wed, he hadn't thought he was. Not until lately. Not until he'd come home one night to find Goldilocks in his bed. Ever since then, his head and his heart had been playing all kinds of wacky tricks on him.

Then again, it could just be that damned comet, he told himself. He was the last person on earth to buy into any kind of cosmic or paranormal hoodoo, but even he had to admit that he sure as hell wasn't acting like himself lately. Maybe, just maybe, there really was something to all this Bob business. Maybe, just maybe, he was under the influence of a celestial disturbance that was playing havoc with his brain.

Or maybe, just maybe, he was actually falling in love with Angie Ellison.

"Ethan?" the woman of his dreams asked beside him, stirring him from his reverie.

"Hmm?" he responded absently, still not quite coherent.

"Aren't you going to open the door?"

He glanced at the brass plaque again. *Honeymoon Suite.* Well, hell, when all was said and done, he supposed he was just as entitled to a honeymoon as anyone else was. If Angie was willing to go through with this counterfeit marriage, then he was, too. It had been his idea, after all. It was necessary if he was going to keep her safe. And no matter what else he had to do during his brief sojourn in Endicott, first and foremost, he intended to keep Angie safe.

As he inserted the key into the door, he found himself wondering just how far she was willing to carry their make-believe marital bliss. Because he was none too strong in his moral convictions where Angie the Angel—not to mention marital bliss—was concerned.

He reminded himself that he'd made a promise to her. Reminded himself that he wasn't supposed to touch her again unless she asked him to. Immediately, he found himself wishing that he really hadn't gone and done something like that. Because, not surprisingly, he really did want to touch Angie again, in all the soft, inviting places he hadn't managed to get to yet.

Of course, with her thinking he was nothing more than a low-life, scumbag, murdering slug, he supposed there was little chance that she would allow him within a good hectometer of herself and all her soft, inviting places. Therefore, all he had to do was come up with some way to make her change her mind.

Piece of cake, right? he thought, thoroughly disgusted with himself. Then again, no one had said marriage would be easy.

He pushed the door open, and as Angie made to precede him into the room, he circled her wrist with strong fingers and held her back. When she spun around and looked up at him curiously, he smiled, then bent to scoop her up into his arms.

"Ethan!" she cried. "What are you doing?"

"I'm carrying my bride over the threshold," he announced, then proceeded to do just that.

Once inside the suite, he kicked the door shut behind them. Vaguely, he noted his surroundings, and saw that the room where the two of them would be spending the next two nights looked exactly like what it was: a honeymoon suite. It was lushly decorated. It was dimly lit. It was, to put it in the vernacular, romantic as all get out.

The room's centerpiece was an intricately carved, antique sleigh bed, its coverlet of ivory lace—conveniently turned back by the housekeeper in anticipation of the bride and groom's arrival—complemented by masses of satin throw pillows scattered at the head. A plush, Oriental rug, larger than any Ethan had ever seen in his life, sprawled across the floor beneath their feet. On an antique buffet against one wall, the management had seen fit to leave a bottle of champagne chilling in a silver ice bucket, alongside a basket of fruit and an assortment of gourmet delicacies the likes of which he wasn't likely to ever see again.

It was a hedonist's dream come true. Expensive wine, delicious food, a bed created for carnal delights and a woman made for exhaustive loving. The good news was that the woman Ethan held in his arms was, in effect—for the time being, anyway—his wife. The bad news was that the only way she wanted to hold him was at arm's length.

He knew he should let her go. Not just from his grasp, but from his life. The situation couldn't be more awkward. He was standing in a room furnished to accommodate insatiable appetites. And he was there with a woman who deserved a hell of a lot more than physical satisfaction.

But instead of settling Angie on her feet, Ethan only pulled her more tightly to him. She met his gaze silently, her eyes filled with a mixture of apprehension and something he decided he'd be better off not contemplating. Because at that moment, with Angie looking at him the way she was looking at him, Ethan could almost believe that the two of them really were husband and wife, in every way that counted.

Except one way, of course. Which, if things worked out as he was beginning to hope they worked out, the two of them were more than likely going to get to in no time at all.

"Okay, I'm over the threshold," Angie said softly when Ethan made no move to relinquish her. "You can put me down now."

She squirmed against him, an action that turned her body in his arms until he had his hand splayed open over her bare back. He skimmed the pad of his thumb over her flesh with a slow, methodical rhythm, marveling at the way her skin seemed to come alive beneath his touch. She was so soft. So warm. So inviting. He didn't think he'd ever met a woman who was softer, or warmer, or even more inviting, than Angie was. And he was helpless to respond to that invitation.

What the hell, he thought. Blame it on Bob, but the only

thing Ethan wanted to do then was make Angie his wife in the most basic, most biblical sense, over and over again. If she told him to shove off, fine. He'd shove off. But if she didn't...

If she didn't, then he was going to see to it that the two of them had the most unforgettable wedding night the world had ever known.

"What if I don't wanna put you down?" he asked her.

Her eyes widened then, but she said nothing in response.

"What if," he added, throwing caution to the wind, "I don't wanna ever let you go?" He hesitated only a moment before emphasizing, "Ever."

Still she remained silent, but where Ethan would have expected her to push him away—either verbally or physically—he felt the arms she had looped around his neck tighten their hold on him, however imperceptibly.

"What if," he continued slowly, "I wanna make our wedding night just that—a wedding night? The way two people who have just been married would normally make their wedding night a wedding night."

Her lips parted as if she intended to tell him something, but she remained silent. Her eyes, however, spoke to him in a way words never could. He saw fear there, true, but he saw something else, as well. Something far more elemental, far more intriguing, far more compelling than fear. He saw desire. He saw need. He saw...love?

"Angel," he began again, not sure what he wanted to tell her, only feeling certain that there was something very important she should know.

When he said nothing more, she swallowed visibly and asked, "What?"

Ethan held her gaze with his, but still couldn't quite summon the words he wanted—needed—to say. He only shook his head slowly, then inched his hand up her back to her neck. He toyed with a few loose tendrils of gold that fell in unruly wisps from the topknot containing the rest of her hair. And he found himself falling more deeply into the dark, bottomless depths of her eyes.

"Angel," he repeated, still feeling woozy and muddle-headed, and in no way certain that he was doing the right thing.

He felt her hands loosen their grip behind his neck, and his heart began to hammer harder as her fingers wandered into his hair and began to fondle the short strands at his nape. A spark of something hot and furious shot through him, and he closed his eyes in an effort to slow the sensation down.

"Yes?" he heard her ask softly.

He squeezed his eyes shut tighter at the sound of her voice, so low and languid and lusty. And he forced himself to focus on whatever it was his brain seemed intent on telling her. Yet still no thoughts jelled in his mind, nor did any words emerge from his mouth.

"Angel," he said again.

"Yes, Ethan?"

He inhaled a deep, unsteady breath and released it slowly, trying to gather his thoughts. "I, um…I, uh…"

"Yes?"

"I…there's something I need to tell you."

"What's that?"

The fingers that had been tripping along his nape scored into his hair, insistently, possessively. He felt Angie dip her head closer to his, her breath stirring the fine hairs at his temple and warming his face. Her heat and her fragrance surrounded him, until he felt as if he were drowning in an endless eddy of emotion. When he snapped his eyes open, it was to find that her mouth was only a hairbreadth away from his own, her lush lips parted slightly in an unmistakable invitation.

"Angel," he said again.

"Ethan, please," she whispered, her voice sounding anxious, needful. "Tell me whatever it is you need to tell me."

And then let's get on with our wedding night.

He didn't know how he knew that was what she was thinking, only that her thoughts almost certainly mirrored his own.

She wanted every bit as badly as he did for this to be their wedding night in the truest sense of the idea, wanted to make love with him as much as he wanted to make love with her. Unmindful of the implications, regardless of the repercussions, damn the torpedoes and full speed ahead.

Comet or no comet.

And he understood then that it really didn't matter to Angie who he claimed to be or what he professed to do for a living. She cared for him. She might possibly even have fallen in love with him. Somehow, she had seen beneath the exterior, beyond the outward image he had been trying so hard to project since coming to Endicott, and she knew—she *knew*—he wasn't the low-life, scumbag, murdering slug he'd tried so hard to assure her he was.

She cared for him, he marveled again. For *him*. She had seen inside, beneath the shell, and she cared for *him*.

He reminded himself that there was something he needed to tell her then, especially if things were going to happen the way he suspected they were going to happen. But for the life of him, he couldn't remember what that revelation could possibly be. He only knew that Angie wanted him, the real him, and he wanted her. So instead of telling her anything, he closed the scant distance remaining between them and kissed her.

Kissed her as if he would never have another chance like this one again.

Because deep down inside, Ethan knew he wouldn't. Once Angie learned the truth about him, once she realized exactly what had brought him to Endicott and recognized the role she was unwittingly playing in the game, she was going to want to flay him alive. So instead of telling her anything that might jeopardize the moment—and he didn't kid himself that this was going to last any more than a moment—he kissed her. Again and again and again.

He slanted his head over hers and covered her mouth with his, taking before she could offer, demanding before she could accommodate. He heard her gasp, felt her stiffen for a moment in his arms at the quickness and ferocity of his invasion. Then, just as quickly, she melted into him, driving the fingers of both hands through his hair, sucking his lower lip into her mouth, taking of him as hungrily as he was her.

Ethan bit back a groan and cupped her nape completely in his palm, dropping his other hand lower to curve his fingers possessively over her fanny. Then he lifted her higher, pulling her closer, so that he could devour her even more voraciously. He drove his tongue into her mouth, moaning when she sucked him in deeper, clutching her more tightly to him when she raked him softly with her teeth. For long moments, they fought to possess each other, their tongues tangled in a dance of desperation, their mouths each vying for domination over the other.

Something hot and explosive shattered Ethan's control then, and he found himself moving toward the bed. But instead of tossing Angie to its center and throwing himself on top of her—which, he had to admit, was what he really wanted to do—he eased himself down on the edge of the mattress and settled her gently onto his lap. But he couldn't make himself stop kissing her.

So, their lips still fused in the most thorough of explorations, he lifted one hand to the coil of hair atop her head and began to search for whatever mysterious means held the rich collection of gold in place. Restlessly, feverishly, he tugged loose one pin after another, discarding them on the floor, until he could cast off her headpiece and free her hair.

When a rush of dark blond curls spilled down around his fingers, he buried both hands in her hair, gripping her head to hold her in place while he plundered her mouth more thoroughly. Angie responded in kind, shifting in his lap until she awkwardly faced him. Then, evidently frustrated with the tight garment that hindered her movements, she released him long enough to hike the skirt of her dress up over her thighs. Then she straddled him, settling each of her knees on the mattress, one on each side of him, tangled her hands in his hair again and kissed him as if her life depended on it.

Ethan couldn't imagine a single good deed he had performed in his entire life that would give him a reward like Angie Ellison. But his thoughts were too fuzzy at the moment even to try to remember. All he could do now was respond to her, enjoying the gift she was offering him, however temporary that gift might be. He roped his arms fiercely around her waist, lest she come to her senses and try to break away from him. Then he leaned back until he felt the softness of the mattress beneath him, bringing Angie along with him for the ride.

Angie wasn't sure what madness had overcome her to make her respond with such need to a man she knew she should consider bad news. But try as she had, she simply could not imagine Ethan as bad in any way. Ever since she'd first encountered him, she had experienced an overpowering uncertainty about him. He had treated her with nothing but tenderness once he'd realized she was no threat to him.

Even having heard him admit that he was exactly the kind of man she had suspected him of being all along hadn't dampened her attraction to him. Even after he'd confirmed her worst fears, she hadn't been able to hate him. She knew it was stupid, and no doubt there were a string of self-help books available for sexy criminals and the women who loved them, but a part of her was convinced that the only thing keeping Ethan from becoming a normal, functioning member of society was the proverbial love of a good woman.

He was smart and funny, warm and gentle, handsome and strong. He was everything she had ever hoped to find in a forever-after kind of man. And try as she might, Angie simply could not abandon a hope she realized now had flickered to life the moment she had kissed him that first night in his bedroom. As much as she had fought it, she still embraced the fervent hope that he could and would go straight for her.

But he's a criminal, a faint voice piped up in some shadowy corner of her brain. *A man whose occupation, whose very lifestyle, stands counter to everything you uphold as true and good.*

No, she responded immediately. Not that. She still didn't know how she could be so certain, but Ethan Zorn was anything but bad.

Then she felt herself falling forward against him, and she ceased to think at all. He was solid and warm beneath her, holding on to her as if she were the answer to every dream he'd ever had, every wish he'd ever uttered. His hands roved hungrily over her bare back, exposed by the deep cut of her gown, into her hair, along her throat. He cupped her cheek gently in one hand, ran his thumb along the line of her jaw, then burrowed into her hair once again. Alternately, he kissed her mouth, her cheek, her neck, her throat. Then he started the ritual all over again.

She had never felt more wanted, more needed, more cherished, more…more loved. It struck her then that Ethan Zorn might very well be a man with whom she could fall in love forever. A wistful, poignant little stab of pain pierced her heart at the realization. Then she forced herself not to think about it.

At the moment, all she wanted was one night with Ethan. One night to forget who he was and why he had come to town. One night to forget who she was, too. One night to hope that maybe things could be different between them. Fifteen years ago, she had wished for something exciting to happen—to Endicott, to herself. And tonight, Bob had seen fit to grant her wish, even if only for a few hours.

Whatever was happening between her and Ethan was inescapable. It was something that had been sealed and ordained fifteen years ago, the moment an adolescent girl had sent her wish skyward. Even if Angie had wanted to stop what was about to happen—and at this point, that was the last thing she wanted to do—she couldn't. Call it fate, call it kismet, call it karma.

Call it comet.

But Angie knew in her heart, could feel in every drop of essence that comprised her, that what was happening now between her and Ethan was, for whatever reason, meant to be.

It was good. It was right. And nothing either one of them could do was going to stop it from coming. So, she decided, they might as well just lie back and enjoy themselves while they could.

After that, she shut down her mind and made herself stop thinking, and focused, instead, on feeling. She nestled her head into Ethan's shoulder and dragged her open mouth along the column of his throat, savoring the hot, salty taste of him on her tongue. The skin she encountered was rough and hard, so very opposite from her own, yet oh, so complementary.

And when he tilted his head to the side to facilitate her exploration, she took advantage of his position to work furiously at the studs fastening his shirt. One by one, Angie loosed the flat, gold disks, tossing them over her shoulder every time she freed one. Little by little, she bared him, skimming her nimble fingers beneath the fabric of his shirt, brushing her lips over him as she went.

When she had freed the garment from the waistband of his trousers, she spread it open wide. As if drawn by some invisible force, her fingers tangled in the dark hair strewn across his chest, effectively imprisoned for the time being. Beneath her fingertips and the soft coils of hair, his skin was warm and satiny. She traced bump after bump of smooth muscle, ridge after ridge of strong sinew. First with her fingers, then with her mouth.

She dipped her head lower, nearing the waistband of his trousers, then covered the buckle of his belt with her hand. Ethan groaned, a feral sound that made her smile against the heated flesh of his flat belly. Then she felt his hands on her shoulders, urging her back up and over his body again, pulling her back to the marauding mouth that had so entranced her earlier. This time, however, Angie was the one who did the deep tasting, penetrating him with her tongue, possessing him with everything else she had to offer.

He palmed her shoulders resolutely, curling his fingers into the stiff, satin fabric of the wedding gown that was already beginning to droop. Before she could say a word to stop him—

not that she wanted to stop him—Ethan was tugging the dress down along her arms. And because the gown was cut so low—both in front and in back—the fabric skidded away in no time at all. Angie pulled her arms free of the lacy sleeves, and he shoved the gown down around her waist.

The feel of his bristly chest nestled against her tender bare flesh sent a wave of keen delight shuddering through her entire system. Instinctively, she rubbed her body along his and heard his gasp of pleasure echo her own. He uttered a rough sound, a mixture of delight and delirium, then covered her bare shoulders with his hands and tried to push her away.

Suddenly and irrationally overcome with shyness, Angie resisted his attempt to gain fuller access to her. But Ethan was insistent. He skimmed his fingers gently down her arms, circling her wrists briefly before pressing his hands against hers, palm to palm. Then he wove their fingers together and began to push her up and away from him. But still she balked, hugging her body close to his in an effort to sabotage his attempt.

"I wanna see you," he murmured in a voice so soft, so seductive, it took every ounce of willpower she had not to give in. "Please, Angel," he said, trying again. "Let me look at you."

For one more moment, she resisted, then she curled her fingers alongside his and let him push her up and away from him. She closed her eyes as she straddled him, trying to quell her rapid respiration, fearing her heart was thundering hard enough to burst. Then Ethan freed her hands, and she felt him trace a line with one finger back up each of her arms, over her shoulders and along her collarbone.

When she finally opened her eyes, she found him staring not at her breasts, but at her face. With his dark gaze locked on hers, he dipped his hands lower, covering each of her breasts. He continued to study her face as he cupped his palms along the lower curves of each breast and touched his thumb to each nipple. Only when he began a slow circular motion across each dusky peak did he lower his gaze to watch his ministrations.

Angie did likewise, her heart pounding even more rapidly at the sight of the two big, masculine hands swallowing her small breasts. His index fingers joined his thumbs then, rolling each of her nipples until they were ripe and full and aching for more. Then, with a gentle squeeze, Ethan raised himself from the mattress to cover one breast with his mouth.

The feel of his tongue against her restive flesh was quite extraordinary, and she closed her eyes at the onslaught of sensation that rocked her. She curled her fingers into his shoulders almost violently, worried he might stop his assault on her senses. But she soon discovered such a fear was unfounded, because Ethan opened his palm over her bare back to bring her closer, sucking her deep into his mouth, tantalizing her first with the flat of his tongue and then with the tumultuous tip.

Angie buried both hands in his hair, then just as quickly skimmed them down to shove his shirt from his shoulders. When Ethan switched his attentions to her other breast, she rose up on her knees to aid him, then tilted her head backward in abandon. Her dress was still bunched around her waist, and his trousers impeded all the things she wanted to do to him. And all she wanted then was to get naked with Ethan.

She pushed him forward again, down onto his back on the bed, then sat back to straddle his waist again. Ethan gazed up at her with wild eyes, his chest rising and falling quickly with ragged gasps for breath. He let his hands wander over her breasts one final time, then circled her waist. And when Angie made a move to unfasten his trousers, he grinned like a satisfied cat.

With Angie on her knees towering over him, with her eyes large and dark with wanting and her bare breasts pink and tumid from his loving, Ethan couldn't keep his hands to himself. As if they had a mind of their own, they roved to the backs of her calves, skimming along the gauzy white silk that encased her legs. Higher and higher his fingers traveled, beneath the hem of her gown, along her slender thighs, until he encountered something that nearly stopped his heart. Garters.

Angie the Angel was wearing a garter belt and stockings. For her wedding day.

For her wedding night.

He remembered then what it was that his brain had been so frantically trying to remind him to tell her. And he knew they couldn't continue with what they were doing until she knew the truth. It would be dangerous. It would be immoral. It might even be illegal. And it would certainly be downright wrong.

"Angel," he said, his voice thready and low. "There's something I have to tell you before we go any further with this."

She smiled at him, but the gesture seemed incomplete somehow. "Seems to me we've gone way too far for revelations now."

He tried to look her in the eye, but his gaze kept straying to the ripe, pink flesh that beckoned to him. "No, this is important," he said, forcing his attention back to her face.

But Angie seemed uninterested in whatever he wanted to tell her, because she reached behind herself to pull down the zipper of his pants. He opened his mouth to object, but she began to toy with the solid ridge of flesh that she encountered when she opened his trousers. Her eyes widened in surprise, though whether her response was due to his size or the fact that he wasn't wearing underwear, Ethan wasn't sure. Maybe a combination of both. At the moment, for some reason, he didn't want to worry about it.

"Angel," he whispered, biting back a groan.

She skimmed her fingertips along the length of him, once, twice, three times. "What?" she asked, her voice a rough whisper.

"I...I, uh...I have to tell you something." God, how he managed to even get those words out with the way she was touching him, he'd never know.

This time she opened her hand completely over him, rubbing the heel of her palm insistently along his eager shaft. "I know everything I need to know," she assured him.

"But—"

"Everything," she repeated.

Before he could say anything more, she released him and leaned over him again, covering his mouth with hers to swallow any words he might have tried to utter. Ethan groaned as his heart started beating double time, and his fingers convulsed on the soft lengths of satin that joined her stockings to the nether regions beneath the wedding gown still hugging her waist.

Fine, he thought. If she refused to listen to reason, then he wasn't even going to try. Angie was a big girl, he reminded himself. And she was just as avid a player in this scene as he was. There would be time for talking later. Right now, both of them had gone too far for conversation anyway.

Later, he told himself again. Later.

Lightly, still strangely fearful she would stop him in spite of her obvious enthusiasm for what was happening between them, he traced the two garters he had encountered up along her thigh. With each of his middle fingers skimming along the length of satin, he trailed his palms along the bare flesh of her legs. It seemed to take forever, but finally, finally, he came to the place where the garters joined with the belt. In between, his fingers found her panties covering the garment, a frothy lace concoction that drew his hands like a magnet.

He deepened their kiss as he pushed aside the whisper of lace that covered her bottom, replacing it with the heels of both hands. With much affection, he molded her firm flesh, palmed her soft cheeks, dipped his fingers into the delicate crease that separated them. He heard her murmur something incoherent against his lips, then felt her grow still atop him.

For a moment, he worried that he had gone too far. Then, ever so slightly, she arched her body until her bottom moved more fully into his grasp. So Ethan ventured farther still, probing her, penetrating her with one swift movement. He heard her gasp, the sound a combination of shock and delight. Then she lowered herself against him again, into the cradle of his thighs.

No longer able to tolerate the few garments left separating

them, Ethan removed his hands from Angie's panties and skimmed them off her bottom, down her thighs and under her knees, discarding them onto the floor. She rose from him long enough to cross her arms over her torso, gripping her gown in her hands, drawing it up and over her head. Ethan used the opportunity to shed his trousers, and then the two of them gazed at each other with frank longing.

"Angel," he said as he gazed at her, trying one more time to make right what might turn out to be so utterly wrong, "before we go any further, I'm tellin' you, there's something you need to know about me. I—"

"Shh," she interrupted him, touching her index finger lightly to his lips. "No, there isn't. I told you. I know everything I need to know about you."

"No, you don't. I—"

"Shh."

"But, Angel—"

She cupped her hand more fully over his mouth and lowered her body back down over his. "Hush."

He circled her wrist with loose fingers and pulled her hand away from his mouth. "But—"

"Make love to me, Ethan. Now."

He studied her for a long, silent moment, torn between his knowledge that she deserved so much more than he was able to give her, and the absolute need to have her that was eating him up inside.

He lowered his gaze to her firm, ripe breasts, to her flat belly, to the curve of her waist and the white length of satin encircling it. Then lower still, to the garters and stockings aligned with her creamy thighs, to the dark-blond thatch of silk in between. And the fingers curling around her wrist clenched convulsively.

Ethan was a strong man—in mind, in body, in self-restraint. But he knew that there was no way he'd ever have the strength or fortitude to resist Angie. Tugging her wrist gently, he pulled her down toward himself again, stifling a groan at the feel of her soft, warm breasts brushing against the solid expanse of his chest.

"Whatever you want, Angel," he heard himself say in a rough voice as he lifted his other hand to wrap his fingers gently around the back of her neck and pull her closer still. "Whatever you want."

Ten

Angie knew it was crazy to be here with Ethan Zorn like this. But it was also as sweet as anything she'd ever experienced before. As he reached for her, she leaned toward him, their movements slow and certain, as if choreographed for an elaborate dance. He curved his fingers around her waist as she threaded hers into his hair. Then he fell backward to the mattress again, pulling her down with him, until she was kneeling over his chest.

What happened next took Angie completely by surprise, silencing her by its very intimacy. Ethan cupped her fanny with insistent hands and pushed her forward, then lowered her to his mouth. As his fingers probed her bottom, his tongue wrought havoc on the tender flesh between her legs. She gasped as she straightened, trying to escape from the onslaught. But Ethan held her firm, gripping her confidently, tasting her with relish.

For a moment, Angie stiffened above him, having never experienced such a sensation in her life. Then quickly, she felt herself melting into him. Unable to find anything else to cling to, she reached for the headboard, her fingers seizing the warm wood as if her life depended on it. Over and over, Ethan assailed her with his mouth, unleashing a wantonness inside her she'd never felt before. And all she could do was close her eyes and surrender—to her feelings, to the sensations rocking her, to Ethan.

"Oh," she murmured. "Oh, Ethan."

Just when she thought the invasion would never end, he pulled her back down toward himself, aligning her body with his. He rolled her to her back and met her gaze levelly with his, covering her breast with one hand.

"You wanted me to make love to you," he reminded her, his dark gaze boring into hers. "And this, Angel..." He closed his fingers over her breast, flicking his thumb against her nipple. Confidently. Possessively. "This is how I make love. Any objections, you better get them out now."

Somehow, she managed to find the strength to shake her head slowly against the pillow beneath it. "No," she whispered weakly. "No objections."

He smiled at her, the gesture turning his expression absolutely predatory. "Good," he murmured, opening his hand over her breast to palm her with much affection.

As he did so, he turned her onto her side, until she lay facing away from him. Angie was about to voice her disappointment at not being able to see him, when she felt him move close behind her. The hard, heavy heart of him speared between her thighs, and her breath caught in her throat at the sheer power she felt burning there. She opened her mouth to gasp for more breath at exactly the same moment he entered her. Deeply, smoothly, irretrievably.

And then she was indeed gasping for breath, and reaching behind herself to loop an arm over his back, holding him exactly where he was. With one hand still curved over her breast, he moved his other to her belly, flattening his palm over her navel before urging his fingers lower. Over and over he furrowed her warm, damp recesses, moving his body against hers, entering and withdrawing, plumbing deeper with every stroke.

Angie grew still as he took possession of her, closing her eyes against wave after wave of euphoria that rocked her. She picked up his rhythm easily, thrusting backward as he moved forward, taking him more completely with every penetration. Time seemed to dissolve into a vague, distant dream, leaving nothing but the feel of Ethan behind and inside her. And just when she thought she would die of the pleasure he wrought within her, he hastened his movements, until, in one incandescent moment, he arched against her, filling her with a white-hot rush of warmth.

They cried out as one at the culmination, the dampness of their bodies mingling and joining both inside and out. A tremor shook Angie from her toes to her fingertips, and she began to shiver uncontrollably. Immediately, Ethan withdrew from her and pulled her close, tugging the covers up over them. For long moments, he only held her close, her dewy back pressed to his slick chest, his lips hovering right above her ear. He whispered meaningless, soothing words that slowly brought her back to reality. Then he carried her to new heights all over again.

This time, though, Angie was the one to lead the dance, casting Ethan as the object of her desires, feasting on him to assuage a hunger gone too long neglected in herself. Their coupling the second time was as fierce as the first, as uninhibited, as demanding, as intense. And, as had been the case the first time, somehow not quite fulfilling.

By midnight, the couple lay tangled in each other's arms, exhausted, spent and fast asleep. Only once did Angie awaken during the night, when Ethan began to mutter something in his sleep about Angels and comets and unwitting salvation. She touched her mouth to his in a soft kiss, and he quieted. Then she snuggled closer, her head pressed to his chest, and listened to the steady thump of his heart beneath her ear.

Ethan awoke with a start to utter blackness, uncertain at first where he was. For one brief instant, terror overtook him, an almost paralyzing fear that he was supposed to be somewhere else, doing something to protect someone he had somehow failed. Then he felt a warm presence by his side, snuggling him, holding him, trusting him. Her soft respiration pressed her body closer to his, and he expelled a ragged breath he hadn't even been aware of holding.

He glanced down, and even in the darkness detected a golden crown of curls that cascaded across his bare chest. Angie. His "wife." His salvation. Bunching a fistful of silky hair in one hand, he lifted it to his lips and closed his eyes tight.

Never, ever, in his entire life, had he ever experienced the kind of response he'd had to making love with Angie Ellison. He wasn't sure when it had happened, or how, but at some point during the night, while the two of them were joined in the most elemental of unions, he had lost a part of his soul—a part of himself—to the woman who lay curled so comfortably at his side.

She should be frightened of him, he thought with something akin to amazement. As far as she knew, he was a criminal— at best a man who flouted the law and social convention, at worst, a Very Bad Man who hurt people. Yet she had surrendered herself to him willingly, had allowed him access to her most intimate secrets, had offered him the most beautiful, most generous gift he'd ever received. Angie the Angel had saved him, to be sure, and from the greatest danger he'd ever known. She'd saved him from himself.

And she didn't even know who he really was.

He swiped a hand over his face and lifted himself on one elbow far enough to get a look at the clock on the nightstand. The glowing round face told him it was 3:48, though whether that was a.m. or p.m. he wasn't able to discern. The honeymoon suite had heavy drapes covering the windows, making it impossible to determine the time of day. He supposed most newlyweds really didn't care much about the passage of time. Then again, most newlyweds hadn't started off their married life on a pack of lies.

Angie slept so soundly he hated to wake her. So he eased his arm out from beneath her as gently as he could, then rolled his body out of bed in silence. Unmindful of his nudity, he padded across the dark room to where he remembered the window being, felt for the drapes and pushed one aside. On the other side of the glass, he saw a black sky shadowed by wispy clouds and studded here and there with stars. He sighed. Only a few hours had passed since he and Angie had consummated their marriage. And already he had regrets.

Not about anything that had happened with Angie. Only about things he had done by himself. And not just recently, either.

Ethan turned his gaze to the black sky, searching in vain for a comet he knew was up there somewhere. "Come out and fight like a man, you bastard," he muttered softly.

But Bob refused to reveal himself, preferring to maintain his mystery under cloak of darkness and cloudy skies while he could wreak his magic on at least one unsuspecting soul.

Ethan wasn't even a resident of Endicott, but he felt as if he'd been whacked by the comet's influence worse than anyone in town. Because nothing else could possibly explain how he could have gone and fallen in love with someone like Angie, so quickly, so completely, so irrevocably.

God, what a mess he'd made of things.

He heard her stir behind him and spun around at the soft sound. For a moment, he thought she would go back to sleep, and he held himself in check, in spite of his desire to go back and join her in bed. Then she sent his name out into the darkness on a whisper-soft sigh, and something tightened in his chest.

"Ethan?"

The quiet sound tore at him, surrounded an emptiness in his heart he hadn't even realized he'd been carrying around—not until he'd come to Endicott, Indiana, and found an Angel waiting for him.

"I'm over here," he told her, his voice just as soft in the darkness as hers was.

He heard her shift in the bed once more, and in the vague darkness, discerned the shape of her rising from it. Then the snap of a lamp washed the room in a pool of pale yellow illumination that seemed almost unearthly somehow. Angie had draped the bed's coverlet around her shoulders, and the rich lace pooled behind her like the train of a wedding gown. Her hair was a riot of gold, her curls spilling down over her forehead and around her shoulders, and her skin seemed paler than he'd ever seen it.

All in all, she looked fragile and innocent and uncertain, and something knotted hard inside him at the realization that he was about to potentially shatter any tenuous chance the two of them might have had at happiness.

"It's freezing in here," she said as she approached him. "Come back to bed."

"Angel, we need to talk."

There, he'd said it. No preamble, no pretense, no preparation at all, but at least the words were out of his mouth. He and Angie really did need to talk. Before things between them went any further than they had. Before things went too far. Without even realizing what he was doing, he sent a silent plea skyward that they hadn't gone too far already.

Angie squinted a bit in the soft light, then shoved a handful of curls off her forehead. "About what?" she asked him.

He suddenly felt uncomfortable in his naked state, so he strode quickly past her, toward the bed again, scooping up his tuxedo trousers from the floor. Strangely, she kept her back to him as he tugged them on, and only when the rasp of the zipper announced that he was clothed—however scantily—did she turn around again. She seemed to tug the coverlet more tightly around herself when she did, and something cool and distant shuttered her eyes.

Honeymoon's over, Ethan thought dryly. Nothing like a strong dose of reality to kill off a perfectly good fantasy.

He inhaled a deep, restless breath, releasing it as he knifed the fingers of both hands through his hair. Then he crossed the room to where Angie stood, and he cupped her cheek in his hand.

"There's something you need to know about me," he told her again.

She shook her head. "No, I told you, I—"

"It's important," he insisted.

"But—"

"Angel," he began. But no other words emerged to further the announcement he knew was so important.

"Ethan, don't. Please don't...."

He could see by the look in her eyes that she didn't want to hear whatever it was he had to tell her, because no matter what the news brought, she knew it was going to change things between them. But she had to know. If the two of them had a hope in hell of salvaging any part of whatever mysterious fire burned between them, she had to know the truth about him. He couldn't keep the secret to himself any longer.

So he met her gaze with every ounce of concentration he possessed, lifted his other hand to cup her neck gently in his palm and stroked the pad of his thumb over her cheek. Once again, he drew a shaky breath, but this time when he expelled it, it was in a rush of words he honestly hadn't even realized he'd spoken until they were out of his mouth.

"Angel, I'm a cop."

The eyes that had been shuttered suddenly went completely blank. She didn't say a word, and for a moment he wondered if she had even heard what he'd just told her. Then another brief, delirious minute passed when he thought she had heard him and everything might be all right. His heart began to hammer happily behind his ribs, and he started to inhale a sigh of relief. Then her focus seemed to sharpen, and she stiffened in his arms. Ethan's heart and breathing skittered to a halt.

"You're what?" she asked, her voice low and level.

He closed his eyes, knowing he was committing a professional sin by what he was about to do, but knowing better that lying to Angie was even worse. "I'm a cop," he repeated, a little more loudly this time.

When he opened his eyes, she was still staring at him, her expression frozen into something Ethan couldn't decide was good or bad. So he pressed onward, hoping for the best, fearing the worst.

"I tried to tell you last night, but you wouldn't let me. I work for the DEA," he said softly. "The Drug Enforcement Agency. I'm sorry, but I don't have any ID to prove that to you right now. I don't carry that kind of thing with me when I'm working undercover the way I have been for the last six months. It could get me killed."

She squeezed her eyes shut at that, and a flicker of hope sputtered to life deep inside him. "So you're just gonna have to trust me on this," he told her.

Her eyes snapped open at that. "Trust you?" she repeated.

He nodded, deciding not to dwell for now on the note of anger he detected in her voice. "The mob thinks I'm working for them. They sent me here to scope out your father's company, and any potential it might have for them to use it as a front for their narcotics trade."

When she said nothing to encourage or dissuade him, Ethan pressed on. But hope slipped further away from him with every word he uttered, because her eyes grew more and more distant every time he opened his mouth.

"I'm *this* close to winding this thing up once and for all, for putting these particular bastards behind bars for a good, long time. If even the slightest thing goes wrong…" He sighed helplessly. "A lot of people could get hurt. Including your family. Including you. And frankly, Angel, I don't think I could handle it if something like that happened."

Still she remained silent, her gaze locked tight on his, her expression revealing nothing about what might be going on in her head. So, heedlessly, hopelessly, Ethan pressed on.

"I swear to you, I never meant for you to get involved in this the way you did, and I never meant for things to go this far. But when you started nosing around, when you wrote those articles for the paper…" He sighed helplessly. "Even if the stories didn't say anything, they put you at risk. Word came down to me from both sides—the mob and the DEA—to do something about you. So I did what I felt was the only thing to do. I panicked, okay? And I faked this marriage for us.''

When she still said nothing, he plodded on again. ''It satisfied the bad guys that you would be true to me and my occupation, and it satisfied the good guys that I could keep an eye on you around the clock. There just wasn't much time for planning anything else.''

He paused for a moment before adding, ''I'm sorry I had to keep you in the dark the way I did. But it was for your own good.''

She studied him in silence for a long time, her eyes never leaving his, her body rigid and unyielding. ''My own good,'' she finally repeated, her voice sounding mechanical, lifeless.

Ethan nodded, but knew he was losing her. ''Yours and your family's. Hell, the whole town's, for that matter.''

She hadn't moved from his grasp, and for one quick moment, in spite of his fear that he had lost her, he thought she might turn toward him instead of away from him. Then slowly, so slowly he could almost convince himself it wasn't happening, she took a step away from him. And where before he had been holding warmth and redemption in his hands, Ethan suddenly found himself clutching nothing but cold night air.

So he, too, stepped forward, closing the distance she had put between them, and reached out for her. Because she was so securely wrapped in the coverlet, he pulled her easily into his arms. Immediately, however, she began to fight him, trying to push him away. Ethan held her as loosely as he could, but refused to let her go. And when her struggles became more insistent, when he came close to losing her completely, he roped his arms more adamantly around her and hauled her against his chest.

''Let me go,'' she snapped, renewing her fight with more ferocity.

''Not until you listen to what I have to say.''

"Let me go," she snarled, twisting her entire body in an effort to free herself.

As much as he hated to comply with her request, he loosened his hold on her enough to let her jerk away from him. But before she could go far, he snagged her wrist in one hand and held on to her, fearing that if he didn't do at least that much, she would bolt right out the door.

"Let me go," she said once more.

He shook his head. "No."

"Ethan—"

"Not until we get a few things settled."

She expelled a single, soft chuckle that was completely lacking in humor. "Oh, right," she said, her voice small and spiritless. "Settled. That's a good one. If we stay here long enough to get anything settled, then we're going to be here for the rest of our lives."

She hadn't met his gaze once since he'd told her the truth about himself, and he didn't like that realization at all. Okay, so maybe he'd just thrown a monkey wrench into a situation that was impossible, but at least now they could work together toward something of a resolution, right? Maybe that resolution was still going to wind up being completely unsatisfactory in a lot of ways, but the two of them weren't at odds anymore. At least, Ethan didn't think they were. Were they?

"Hey, staying here with you for the rest of my life would suit me just fine," he told her.

She laughed again, the sound hollow and joyless. "Yeah, I bet it would."

He shook his head at her and tightened his hold on her wrist, still fearful she would abandon him. "Look, I know this comes as a shock to you, and I know it changes a lot of things. But why the hell are you so angry?"

Her eyebrows shot up at that. "Why am I angry?" she echoed. "Why am I *angry?*"

He nodded. "I would think you'd be relieved to discover I'm not the low-life, scumbag, murdering slug you thought I was. Not after…"

He swallowed hard, unable to bring himself to vocalize what had happened between them only a few hours ago. It was still too fresh, too new, too raw an emotion for him to deal with. Evidently, Angie couldn't quite put words to it, either, because she lowered her gaze to the floor and pretended not to know what he was talking about.

Instead, she only stiffened at the memory he had obviously roused in her, too, and said softly, "I haven't thought that about you for some time." When she glanced up at him again, her eyes were bright and damp. "I wasn't sure what you were, but I knew you weren't a bad guy."

Now Ethan was really confused. "Then why does the fact that I'm a cop change anything?"

"Because it means you've been lying to me all along. It means you're a liar."

He gaped at her. "You liked me well enough when you thought I was a felon. Don't tell me few white lies are going to change anything."

"White lies?" she repeated. "This goes way beyond a few white lies."

"In what way?"

She glared at him, clearly unable to understand his confusion. Then she gave her wrist a good, swift tug that freed her from his grasp. Thankfully, however, she didn't move to escape. He didn't know what he would have done if she'd tried to flee.

She rubbed fiercely at her eyes with thumb and forefinger, then scrubbed a knuckle under her nose. Her other hand still clutched the bedclothes around her body, tightening with every word she spoke, as if she were wielding a shield.

"Don't you get it?" she demanded when she finally returned her attention to him.

He shook his head again, honestly mystified by her outrage. He'd known she would be upset by the news that he wasn't who he'd claimed to be—neither a traveling sales rep, nor a front man for the mob. But he thought that upset would come from her own shock and confusion about the situation. And he'd assumed that once the initial shock and confusion wore off, she'd be delighted to discover that the man she'd just traded body fluids with was at least on the right side of the law.

Then he remembered something else. They really had just traded body fluids. Fluids that were potentially life generating. They hadn't used any kind of barrier to prevent something like…oh…a baby, for example. Oh, no. Oh, jeez. Oh, great.

Okay, so now maybe he could understand why she was so mad. Sort of. Or maybe not. Maybe they still weren't quite following the same wavelength.

"No," he told her tentatively. "I don't think I do get it. Maybe you could spell it out for me."

"Oh, you got it, all right," she snapped. "That's the problem. You got just what you wanted. A nice, little tumble and a nice, little piece. From me."

He shook his head vehemently. "No, Angel, that's not it at all. Whatever…whatever *happened* here tonight, it went way beyond 'getting it.'" He thrust a thumb over his shoulder, toward the bed, but his gaze lingered on hers. "Nothing like that has ever happened to me before," he assured her. "And I can't see it ever happening again. Not unless I'm with you when it happens."

"That's not likely to happen."

He dropped his hand back to his side. Somehow, he'd known she was going to say that, regardless of how she took the news of his real identity. Nonetheless, it still hurt to hear the words spoken.

"Why not?" he asked her, hating the desperate quality his voice seemed to have adopted.

Her eyebrows arrowed down this time, and she sniffled softly. "Because, Ethan, you're a liar."

He still didn't understand. "You don't mind making love with a man who breaks the law, but you draw the line at someone who doesn't tell the truth?"

She nodded slowly.

"Angel, that makes absolutely no sense."

She stared at him as if he were the biggest moron she'd ever had the misfortune to meet. "Of course it makes sense. It makes perfect sense."

"No, it doesn't."

She wrapped the bedspread more tightly around her and met his gaze levelly, but her eyes were still wet with unshed tears, and her posture was still limp and defeated.

"Ethan the felon, in spite of being a felon, was a man I thought I could trust. He was a man I thought trusted me."

"Oh, Angel—"

"But Ethan the cop is a stranger," she interrupted him. "Someone who didn't trust me enough to tell me the truth right away."

"I couldn't, don't you understand? If I had told you who I was—"

"And as a result," she cut him off again, "Ethan the cop is someone I can't trust."

He stared at her in silence for a minute, then expelled a growl of exasperation. "This is crazy. I can't believe you cared about me when I was on the wrong side of the law, but now that I'm back on the right side, you don't think I can be trusted."

"I know it sounds crazy to you, but it makes perfect sense to me."

It *would* make perfect sense to her, he thought. Nothing Angie Ellison had said or done since he'd first found her in his bed had fallen anywhere close to socially or psychologically sound.

Once again, she tugged at the coverlet with all the imperiousness of a queen. "Now, if you'll excuse me," she said as she took a few steps toward him, "I have some packing to do. I'm leaving. This honeymoon is over. This marriage is kaput."

As she passed him, he reached for her again, cupping her shoulder securely before spinning her around to face him. "Oh, no, it's not," he assured her. "You're not going anywhere."

When she tried to spin away from him again, he clapped his other hand over her other shoulder and held her fast. Her dark eyes glittered with the fire of combat, but he didn't budge an inch.

"Let…me…*go*," she commanded through gritted teeth.

"It's our honeymoon," he reminded her. "We have this room for another day and another night. You leave now, people are gonna wonder why. They're gonna think maybe this marriage isn't all it's cracked up to be. They're gonna think maybe it was *arranged.* And some of them are gonna get scared that maybe they can't trust you to do the right thing after all where your hubby's occupation is concerned."

He adopted his best Marlon Brando voice once again. "In short, Angel, somebody might get spooked that you're running out on your husband, and that somebody might get it into his head that you'd be better off…offed. You know what I'm sayin' here?"

She eyed him narrowly. "Knock off the *Maltese Falcon* shtick," she told him. "I'm not falling for that one again."

"That was *The Godfather,* not *The Maltese Falcon,*" he told her dryly. "And it's no shtick. You need protecting, and I'm here to do it. You leave now, and it's gonna be open season on nosy blond journalists. This marriage has to look exactly like a marriage. In every sense of the word."

He dropped his hands back to his sides, but still didn't trust her not to bolt. As an added incentive, he told her, "Whether you like it or not, your life is in danger unless I'm standing right by your side. And that means you're stuck in this room for another good thirty hours. With me. And then, Angel, we're going home together. To my home. To *our* home. As man and wife. And we'll remain man and wife until I wind this investigation up once and for all."

He strode past her toward the buffet and reached for the magnum of champagne that still lay chilling in a bucket of limp ice. He forced a bravado he came nowhere near feeling, still terrified she was going to walk out the door and into the line of fire. If he had to tie her up again, he would, he thought.

Hopefully, however, that wouldn't be necessary. With any luck at all, maybe he could resort to other, more enjoyable, ways to cajole her around to his way of thinking.

He plucked the big bottle of champagne out of its nest amid the crunch and clinking of ice cubes. "Dom Pérignon," he said over his shoulder as he read the label. "Good stuff." Then he bent down toward the mini-refrigerator beside the buffet and slung the door open wide. "Oh, goody, and orange juice, too," he added.

He straightened, holding champagne in one hand and a carton of Minute Maid in the other. "So what say, Angel? We're coming up on morning. You in the mood for mimosas or what?"

Eleven

Angie stared at the stranger she had fancied herself falling in love with and wondered what to do now. Ethan still looked and sounded the same as he had before. He walked the same way and talked the same way that he had before. His dark eyes were still depthless and full of the troublemaker, yet still reminiscent of an orphaned fawn. Half-dressed as he was—or perhaps half-naked, depending on whether one was a pessimist or an optimist, she supposed—he still sent her heart and her libido racing double time.

Damn him.

But he wasn't the same man, she insisted to herself. He wasn't the criminal with a heart of gold who had roused so many conflicting, confounding emotions in her. He wasn't the rebel with a lame cause. He wasn't a fallen angel in need of redemption. He wasn't the bad guy who might be saved by the love of a good woman. He just wasn't the Ethan Zorn she had come to know and love.

Was he?

When she made no response to his offer of mimosas, he shrugged negligently and turned his back to make them anyway. She watched the play of muscles along his bare back and arms as he opened both champagne and orange juice and poured equal amounts of each into two wine stems. Her gaze fell lower, lingering at the taut derriere, the long legs, the sexy feet, and she was helpless to prevent the wistful longing that wound through her.

He was so handsome, she thought when he turned back around and began a slow, methodical approach toward her, armed with a glass in each hand. As he drew nearer, she hastily replayed their union of only hours ago. He had made love to her with such passion, such intensity, such care. He had made her feel as if maybe he had fallen for her as completely and irredeemably as she had fallen for him. She had begun to think he loved her. Had begun to think maybe she loved him, too.

Regardless of what kind of man he professed to be.

Because no matter what he had claimed of himself, she had seen something else in him, something that went much deeper than an occupation or a lifestyle. She had seen that he was a good, decent man, in spite of his assurances and her own suspicions to the contrary. So why was she so surprised to find out that he wasn't a mobster at all, that he was working on the right side of the law to put such people away? And why was she so outraged by the discovery?

He halted his forward progress when there was still a good ten inches of space and absolutely no answers between them. Then, silently, he extended a wineglass toward her. She took it from him automatically and lifted it to her lips for an idle sip. The concoction was sweet and light and effervescent, so utterly different from the turbulent emotions swirling in her heart.

They'd been married less than a day, she mused, and already he was driving her to drink.

"So you think Ethan the cop is a stranger?" he asked after a taste of his own drink.

Silently, because she wasn't certain she could muster the words she needed to speak, she nodded.

"You think I'm a different man from the one you fell in love with?"

Again, she nodded mutely.

He smiled, a satisfied, certain smile. "Then you admit you're in love with me?"

Oh, smooth, she thought. Very smooth. Way to trip her up. "I admit that I fell in love with a man who said his name was Ethan Zorn," she confessed. "But I don't love *you.* I can't possibly love a stranger."

His smile faltered some, but he rallied it well. "Then I guess we need to get to know each other better."

Before she could say anything to object, he extended his free hand toward her. "Ethan Zorn," he said mildly. "Male. Caucasian. Thirty-four years old. Capricorn. Birthplace, Philadelphia, Pennsylvania. Graduate, Eisenhower High School and Penn State University. My parents died when I was fourteen, and I was raised after that by two older brothers who also still live in South Philly. I survived all the normal childhood illnesses, and I had to get three stitches in my chin when I was two years old. My favorite color is blue. I love Italian food, driving fast and weekends at the shore."

When Angie refused to take his hand, his smile fell some more, and he dropped his hand to settle it on his hip. But his eyes never left hers.

"Oh, and I work for the DEA," he continued. "I've come to Endicott to investigate some strange goings-on that involve Ellison Pharmaceuticals. Sorry, but I can't go into particulars. And your name is…?"

She told herself to ignore his attempt at levity, to pack her bags and leave, regardless of any implied threat to her safety that might be waiting for her on the other side of the honeymoon suite. Wrapping the bedspread more securely around herself, however, she found herself replying, "Angie Ellison. My father owns Ellison Pharmaceuticals."

Ethan smiled at her, and for a moment, she thought she

detected something of the man she had indeed fallen in love with.

It's not him, she tried to assure herself. *This man is a stranger. A liar. A user.*

Unfortunately, she realized quickly that she wasn't falling for that argument at all.

"Nice to meet you, Angie."

It was the first time he had called her by her name, instead of the nickname he had adopted for her when he was a criminal. And oddly enough, she was actually disappointed to hear him use it. She couldn't imagine why—she'd never liked being called "Angel" to begin with. But having Ethan refer to her as "Angie" now only reinforced the reminder that he wasn't the man she had thought him to be.

Then again, she asked herself, was that really such a terrible thing?

Yes, it's most definitely a terrible thing, she answered herself immediately. *Because it means that he's been lying to you and using you since the moment you met him.*

It also meant he wasn't a criminal. He wasn't one of the bad guys.

Then again, "good" and "bad" are both relative terms, she argued with herself.

Not necessarily. Not in this case, anyway.

Angie shook her head at the strange disagreement she was launching with her own brain and tried to focus on the situation at hand. That situation being that she had just discovered that a man she thought she loved was actually someone she didn't know at all.

Someone who was also trying to rectify that situation, if she would only give him a chance.

"So, Angie," he said after another sip of his drink. "Tell me a little bit about yourself."

She sighed halfheartedly. "What's there to tell?"

"Did you grow up around here or what?"

The South Philly accent that had permeated Ethan the felon's speech was still very much present in Ethan the cop's voice, and that, at least, made her smile. "Yes, I grew up in Endicott," she told him, wondering why she was even bothering with this game. He was still a liar. Nothing was going to change that fact.

He nodded. "I grew up in Philadelphia," he told her. "South Philly. *Great* neighborhood. You'd love it there."

She scrunched up her shoulders awkwardly. "I like it here just fine," she said, amazed to realize that the assertion was true.

All these years, she'd cursed Endicott for being so sleepy and boring. All these years, she'd wanted nothing more than to have something exciting happen to the little town. Now that she'd had a taste of more than enough excitement, she decided there was a lot to be said for sleepy and boring. She had no doubt that there were far more eventful—far more *exciting*—places to live than her hometown. But for the first time in her life, she realized she simply did not want any part of them.

"Okay," Ethan conceded when she offered nothing else. "I admit you got a nice community here, regardless of that little mob problem. But we're working on that." He toddled his head back and forth in thought. "All in all, this wouldn't be such a bad place to settle down, I guess. Start a family. That kind of thing. Once we get rid of the mob, I mean."

Little by little, Angie felt her resentment toward the man dissolving, regardless of how much she tried to preserve it. "You, uh, you're sure you're going to rout the little buggers?" she asked him.

"Yeah, you bet."

"And once you do," she said quietly, "I guess you'll be leaving. Going back to Philadelphia."

He studied her for a long moment, then shook his head. "Not necessarily."

Something warm and wishful bubbled up inside her, so she tried to force it back down. "Why on earth would you want to stay someplace like this?" she asked him.

He shrugged. "Why would you?"

"Because I live here," she told him. "It's where I grew up.

My family is here." She met his gaze levelly. "Endicott is my home. It's where I belong."

"Maybe it's where I belong, too."

She thought about that for a minute, turned it over in her head a number of times. Ethan in Endicott. As a member of the community instead of a threat to it. Interesting concept.... She honestly couldn't remember the last time someone new had moved to town to stay. Endicott was a nice place, but it wasn't a mecca of opportunity people flocked to in droves.

It didn't matter, she told herself. Whatever Ethan did or didn't do now was immaterial, because he wasn't the man she had thought him to be. He wasn't the man she had fallen in love with. He was a stranger. A stranger with whom she had done things, she recalled now as a sexual heat rushed through her, that she would *never* have done under normal circumstances. A stranger she had fancied herself in love with, a stranger she had fallen for without thought because a comet that was just passing through had played a little joke on her.

It was Bob, Angie reminded herself. This entire sorry mess was all Bob's fault. Bob's galactic disturbances had messed with her perception and caused her to fall for Ethan in the first place. And Bob would be on his way out of town in a couple of days, restoring the cosmos to its proper balance. Once the comet had left Endicott, everything would go back to normal again. And normal did not include Ethan Zorn in any way, shape or form. Neither Ethan the felon, nor Ethan the cop.

Arguing with herself was pointless. Conversing with Ethan was pointless. This whole thing was little more than a bad melodrama played out for a comet's entertainment. How could she have let herself forget that?

"It's no good, Ethan," she said softly. "It won't work."

The hopeful look that had begun to dawn on his face suddenly turned dark. "What do you mean?"

She sighed heavily and jerked the bedspread up around her shoulders again. "I mean none of this matters," she told him. "It doesn't matter whether you stay in Endicott or not. It doesn't matter whether you're Ethan the felon or Ethan the cop. It doesn't matter whether you're a liar or not.''

''Angie, I told you—I'm *not* a liar. I couldn't reveal my true identity to you—it could have gotten both of us killed. If you'll just be patient for a few more days, until I can—''

''In a few more days,'' she interrupted, ''Bob will be gone from Endicott and we won't be under his influence anymore. We'll stop feeling the way we've been feeling. I won't love you anymore—either of you. And you—'' Her voice broke off in a sad little hiccup. She cleared her throat with some difficulty and finished. ''Neither of you will love me. If either of you ever really did to begin with. Which I sincerely doubt.''

''Oh, Angie.'' He shook his head vehemently. ''Angel. There's only one of me. And I do love you. That's what I've been trying to tell you. I think I've loved you from the minute I found you breaking into my house. And nothing will ever change that. It's not a comet thing,'' he assured her with a sad smile. ''It's a cupid thing. I love you. And I'll do whatever it takes to make sure nothing happens to us. That's all there is to it.''

She wished she could believe him. With all her heart, she wished she could trust that what he said was true. But there were so many factors at play here, and so few of those factors were within their control. The two of them had met at the worst possible time, and under the worst possible conditions. There was Ethan's undercover status, his unresolved investigation, a threat to Angie's safety that might or might not be real. There were falsehoods, subterfuges, obfuscations. There was so much left undecided, unsettled and unknown.

And then, of course, there was Bob. A wild card if ever there was one.

''Ethan, how can you know anything at this point?'' Angie asked him. ''There's so much confusion and uncertainty at this stage of the game I hardly know my own name, let alone your intentions.''

He laughed, an anxious, despondent sound. ''I know I love

you," he said. "And I know nothing will ever change that. That's enough for me."

"Well, it's not enough for me," she said softly. "I'm sorry, but I can't be nearly as sure about all this as you are. It's just too much to handle. There's too much gone wrong to ever make it all right."

He took a step toward her, and even though her instincts told her to dart away, Angie stood firm. But when he cupped her jaw in his warm, rough hand, when he traced his thumb gingerly over her delicate cheekbone, she felt herself swaying toward him.

"Like I told you earlier," he said, his voice a murmur, "we have a good thirty hours to spend locked up together in this room. Thirty hours to get this all ironed out." He pulled her forward until he could dip his forehead to press it against hers. "Thirty hours," he added, "for me to convince you once and for all of who I am and what I feel for you."

She shook her head sadly. "It's not enough," she told him again. "Thirty years wouldn't be enough, let alone thirty hours."

He nodded certainly. "Thirty hours will be more than enough. Let me show you."

Before she could respond one way or another, he dipped his head lower and covered her mouth with his. This time when Ethan kissed her, it was as it had never been before. Gone was the unleashed passion, the uncontrolled desire, the desperation and need. Instead, there was solicitude and softness, petition and promise. His mouth, his kiss, was gentle and tender, and oh, so very convincing. Which was all the more reason, Angie knew, that she had to put an end to it now.

"No, Ethan," she whispered as she pulled away. When he bent forward as if to kiss her again, she covered his mouth loosely with her hand. "No more. Please. I can't. I just...I can't."

Her plea stopped him cold. He took a step away from her and spun around, hooking his hands on his hips, hanging his head in defeat. "You still can't leave this room yet," he told her softly. "Neither one of us can. It wouldn't look good. I'll sleep on the couch tonight if it comes to that, and you can have the bed. But for the next thirty hours, Angie, we're stuck together."

His announcement and capitulation both stated, he strode across the suite to the bathroom. Then he closed the door and locked it, and the sound of rushing water told her all she needed to know. He was washing his hands of her. Literally and figuratively. And why the knowledge of that didn't reassure her more, she couldn't begin to understand.

So she sipped her mimosa, grimacing when she realized that the champagne had already gone flat. Then she riffled a hand through her hair and strode to her still-packed suitcase to find some clothes.

Thirty hours trapped with Angie wound up being more like three. Shortly after the sun crept over the horizon, the phone on the nightstand rang shrilly, punctuating with urgency an already taut situation. Ethan let it ring four times before picking up the receiver, because he honestly didn't want to hear whatever whoever had to say.

"Zorn," he answered shortly as he settled the receiver against his ear.

On the other side of the room, Angie sat on the couch with her back to him, staring at a novel she'd had the foresight to pack for her honeymoon. She'd been there when he'd exited the bathroom after his shower, and had returned to the position immediately after completing her own toilette. She'd neither spoken to, nor looked at, him once, and he was beginning to wonder if she had fallen asleep sitting up. But when she turned her head slightly toward him, clearly with the intent to eavesdrop on his conversation, he realized she was more interested in her immediate surroundings than she was letting on.

"So, Romeo, you ever gonna come outta that room, or are we gonna have to come in and get you?"

Venturi. A slight improvement over Palmieri, but still a low-life, as far as Ethan was concerned, regardless of the fact that Vic Venturi also worked for the DEA.

"I'm kinda busy right now, Vic," Ethan told him.

"Yeah, I would be, too, if I had a wife what looked like yours." A dry wheeze somewhat reminiscent of laughter erupted over the line. "Sometimes the perks of the job ain't so bad, huh?"

"What do you want, Venturi?" Ethan asked wearily. "I thought I could at least enjoy my honeymoon before I heard from you guys."

The other man chuckled once or twice more, then sobered. "It's goin' down earlier than we planned."

Something tightened in Ethan's midsection, and he turned his attention back to Angie, who was still listening in on the conversation. "How much earlier?"

"Forty-five minutes from now."

Ethan gaped at the telephone receiver. "Forty-five minutes? How the hell did that happen? It was supposed to be in three days."

He heard the shrug in Vic's voice. "Leo got itchy. Moved too fast at his end of things. All these wise guys in town for your wedding, we shoulda figured something like this was gonna happen. Now we gotta go in and make sure everything goes down the way it's supposed to. Just a lot earlier than we planned. You need to be at Ellison Pharmaceuticals in a half hour. Everything else is gonna go exactly according to plan. Happy honeymoon."

And then the line went dead. Great, Ethan thought as he dropped the receiver back into the cradle. This was just great. He'd known everything was coming to a head, maybe even a little faster than things were supposed to. But he'd anticipated they still had at least a couple of days to get things in place before they had to move in on everybody.

He glanced down at his watch, then back up at Angie. At least she would be safe, he told himself. And maybe now that the investigation was drawing to a close, the two of them could focus on more important things.

Like spending the rest of their lives together.

"Angie," he said softly.

He had halfway expected her to ignore him, to return her attention to the book she'd been pretending to read. But instead, she altered her position on the couch until she had turned around to face him.

"What?" she asked.

In her black leggings and oversize red sweatshirt, with big red socks on her feet and her hair piled into a loose ponytail atop her head, she looked beautiful and warm and welcoming. All he wanted to do was go over and join her on the couch, and show her again how very much he loved her.

Unfortunately, he had a job to do first, and the realization of that lurched him into action. He moved to the closet and withdrew one of his signature dark suits, and began to quickly unfasten the buttons of his flannel shirt as he spoke.

"I gotta go out," he said simply.

She didn't seem surprised by the announcement, but her eyes darkened with concern. "I thought you said we had thirty hours."

He shrugged, his shirt falling from his shoulders into his hands. "I was wrong."

"What happened?"

He pulled a white dress shirt on in place of the flannel and hastily buttoned himself up. "I can't go into details. But my law enforcement connections tell me we have to move the timetable up a bit. It'll all be over in a few hours."

She looked more worried at that, her forehead furrowing in a frown that mirrored the one turning down her mouth. "What will all be over?"

He smiled at her, hoping his expression was reassuring, then went to work on his jeans. "The investigation, that's all."

She nodded, but seemed more interested in watching him undress than she was in what he had to tell her. "Will you be coming back to the hotel?" she asked, her voice a bit shallow, a bit uneven.

He shook his head, cast off his jeans and stepped into his

suit trousers. "I'm gonna have to stay on scene for a while. Then I'll have some paperwork to do. It could be some time before I'm finished."

She rubbed at the furrows on her forehead, then met his gaze levelly. "Will you…" She sighed heavily. "Ethan, will you be…okay?"

He jerked a necktie from a hanger and flipped up the collar of his shirt, then smiled at the obvious concern lacing her voice. There was still a chance, he realized. There was still some hope that she would come around and realize that neither of them could fight what was happening to them, that comet or no comet, their fates were entwined irrevocably and indefinitely.

"Don't worry about me, Angel," he assured her. "I've got a lot invested in this."

"I know," she answered coolly. "You have six months' worth of undercover work invested."

He shook his head, his smile broadening. "No, I've got more than that invested here. A hell of a lot more than that. I'll be back. Don't you worry."

She said nothing to that, just continued to hold his gaze and study his face as if she were trying to commit it to memory.

"Stay here in the hotel room until you hear from me," he told her when he finished dressing.

"Am I in any kind of danger? Is my family?"

"No," he told her, confident that was true. "Everything's fine. But I'd feel better if I knew where you were. Just wait until I call you before you go home, okay?"

She nodded. "Okay."

"Oh, and Angel?"

"Yes?"

"Remember that I love you."

Before she could respond, he leaned forward and kissed her again—hard and fast. Then he cupped her cheek gently in his palm one final time and drank in the sight of her dark eyes, so full of something that made his heart race faster. Then he forced himself to move away from her, through the door inscripted so beautifully with the words *Honeymoon Suite,* and went to meet a man.

Twelve

Ethan called the hotel room a little more than five hours after he left it. When Angie answered the phone, his voice and words were cool, detached, professional. Yes, everything went down according to plan. Yes, the guys they wanted to put behind bars were safely locked away from polite society. Yes, her family and her father's company were perfectly okay. Yes, he was perfectly fine, too. Yes, Angie could go home now.

And no, he wouldn't be able to see her before he left for Philadelphia, because he had to return right away to straighten out some aspects of the case. But, hey, he'd call her just as soon as he could, he promised, because the two of them had a lot of talking to do.

Why the thought of him leaving hit her so hard, Angie couldn't imagine. It wasn't as if she'd actually wanted to see him before he left, she told herself. That would have just made things worse. No, the two of them were much better off making a clean break of it. No sense putting off the inevitable.

The inevitable being that they would go their separate ways and live their separate lives.

What else could they do? she asked herself as she let herself into her apartment Sunday evening and dropped her suitcase onto the floor. This was exactly what she'd expected, wasn't it? Even if Ethan's reasons for having to leave were job related, he'd still had to leave. And he would have left, no matter what. Because that's just the way fate worked.

Bob had granted Angie's wish. He'd brought some excitement to town. And now that Bob was on his way out, he was taking that excitement with him.

She didn't kid herself that Ethan would be back. Once he returned to Philadelphia, he'd be outside the comet's influence, and he'd realize that his feelings for her weren't what he'd originally perceived them to be. He'd realize he didn't actually love her. And once Bob moved completely beyond Endicott, which he would be doing in a matter of days, Angie, too, would stop feeling so enamored of Ethan and be able to go on with her life.

She should be relieved that things were going to finally get back to normal, she told herself. So why did she feel so empty and forlorn, instead?

"Must be comet hangover," she muttered as she closed her front door and leaned back against it. No doubt a couple of aspirin would clear it right up.

On Monday, Angie told her parents that Ethan was called away on work, deciding to reveal her impending and inevitable divorce later, when she was more able to deal with it herself. Then she returned to work feeling no better about the way things had turned out than she had upon Ethan's departure the day before. He still hadn't called her, nor did she expect him to. She *wanted* him to call, she realized without much surprise, but she didn't *expect* him to. Because he didn't love her anymore. And in a few days, she was certain, she wouldn't love him, either.

On Tuesday, she woke up with the cramps and was oddly upset by the knowledge that her impromptu union with Ethan hadn't resulted in pregnancy. This in spite of the fact that she'd known full well at the time that she was nowhere near her fertile period in her cycle. This in spite of the fact that the last thing she wanted to find herself being was a single mother. This in spite of the fact that she was certain her love for Ethan was only temporary anyway. So what was the big deal, right?

On Wednesday, she dialed information in Philadelphia and requested the phone number of one Ethan Zorn, only to be told by a cold, mechanical voice that the listing wasn't available for public consumption. But that was okay, she told herself as she hung up the phone, because it would have been pointless to talk to him anyway. Bob was gone, and soon her lingering fondness for Ethan would be, too. Then she microwaved a frozen pizza for dinner and left it untouched on her plate.

On Thursday, she stopped at the video store on the way home from work and rented the original *Scarface* and *An Affair to Remember*. Then she stayed up until 3 a.m. waiting for the phone to ring. It didn't. But of course, that didn't surprise her, because by now Ethan had probably forgotten all about her. And surely by tomorrow, she would forget all about him, too. Bob's exit from Endicott was official now, and his cosmic influences would be wearing off any minute. She just needed to be a little more patient, that was all.

On Friday, after sharing a celebratory lunch with a recently engaged friend, Angie came home, snuggled up with the heating pad and a cup of chamomile tea and cried. According to amateur and professional astronomers alike, Bob was well and truly gone, far beyond the earth's orbit, nowhere near Endicott, making his way happily toward the sun.

And she was still in love with Ethan. A love that had diminished in no way, shape or form since his or Bob's departure. A love that had instead settled deep into her soul. A love she knew would never go away, no matter where Bob—or Ethan—chose to travel.

On Saturday, when Angie woke up, she decided to stay in bed for the rest of her life. What was the point of getting up anyway, she reasoned, when you were just a stupid idiot who couldn't see the most obvious thing in the world? When you were dumb enough to think something as powerful as love could be faked by a comet's influence? When you were so blind, you let the most wonderful man you'd ever met slip away?

Of course, Ethan would have left anyway, she assured herself ruthlessly, regardless of her feelings for him. Because even though *she* hadn't been moved by Bob's influences where her feelings for Ethan were concerned, Ethan obviously *had* been overcome by Bob. Otherwise, he would have at least called her by now. And now that he was no longer under the influence, so to speak, he had come to his senses and forgotten all about his cosmic experience in Endicott.

Angie wished she could say the same about herself.

Instead, she ignored the laughter of children and the songs of the birds outside the open window, rolled over to her stomach and yanked the covers up over her head. If she tried very hard, she thought, maybe she could get a really good bout of self-pity going, and then she'd have an excuse to binge on Snickers ice cream for breakfast. Come to think of it, though, she thought as her eyes burned with tears and her throat knotted roughly, that self-pity stuff probably wasn't going to be tough to manage at all.

She was just about there when someone jerked the sheet away from her, exposing her to the light of day. Angie gasped and rolled over onto her back, shoving her hair out of her eyes as she did so, and found herself gazing into the most delicious pair of brown eyes she had ever seen.

"Yo, Angel," Ethan said, his eyes merry, his smile genuinely delighted. "What's new?"

She pushed herself up to a sitting position and rubbed her eyes. Then she left her hands where they were and counted slowly to three. When she moved them and opened her eyes again, Ethan was still there. Her gaze roved quickly and hungrily over him, taking in the faded jeans that molded his legs, the baggy, oatmeal-colored sweater that did nothing to hide the breadth of his shoulders and the tautness of his belly, the dark hair ruffled by the autumn wind that shook the apartment building from outside and billowed the curtains above her bed.

"Ethan?" she asked uncertainly, in spite of the physical evidence right there within her reach.

He spread his arms open wide, his smile growing broader as he did so. "None other than."

"Wh-what are you doing here?"

He dropped his hands to his sides, then immediately seemed to reconsider the posture and leaned forward to place one on each side of Angie, instead. "That's something we need to talk about," he said softly. "Just because the mob doesn't live here anymore doesn't mean you can leave your doors unlocked."

"But nothing ever happens in Endicott," she replied automatically.

He wiggled his eyebrows playfully. "That's a matter of opinion." He leaned forward more, until his forehead was nearly touching hers. "Last time I was in town, I fell in love and got married. I wouldn't call that 'nothing.'"

Something warm and bubbly rippled through her, and she remembered that she was still in her nightshirt. Still in bed. Still aching for Ethan. Then again, she decided, that might not be such a bad position to be in at that.

She lifted a hand to cup his rough jaw and sighed heavily with relief. "Oh, Ethan. Are you sure? Do you still love me?"

"Now *that,* Angel, is a stupid question. Of course I love you."

"But Bob's gone," she reminded him, wondering why she was bothering to argue with him over something she'd been longing to hear him say. "And you never called me. I thought for sure you'd—"

"The comet may be gone," he interrupted her, "but my love for you is still here, and I can tell you right now that it's not going anywhere. That's something you *can't* blame on Bob," he told her. "The reason I didn't call was that I wanted to give you time to realize you love me, too, comet or no comet.'' His smile faltered some. ''You, uh, you do still love me, don't you?''

''Oh, Ethan.'' She sighed again, curving her other hand over his other cheek, framing his face in her palms. ''Of course I love you.''

His grin turned smug. ''It's about time you came clean with that.'' He eyed her thoughtfully for a moment. ''You sure you're not going to try to blame it on Bob?''

She chuckled. ''No, what I feel for you definitely comes from the heart. My heart. I wouldn't think of giving Bob credit for that.''

Ethan nodded satisfactorily. ''Good. Um, there is one thing, though, Angel, that you should know.''

She threaded the fingers of one hand into his hair, and started to pull him close. ''Hmm?'' she asked dreamily. ''What's that?''

''You remember that little wedding we had last weekend?''

She nodded, urging him closer still. ''How could I forget?''

He let himself be pulled down to the bed with her, angling his body next to hers, roping one arm around her waist. Then he lifted a hand to her shoulder and toyed with the neck of her gray fleece nightshirt, skimming the pad of his thumb along the length of her collarbone and back again.

''That wedding?'' he asked again. ''It, uh… It was, um… It was legal. And binding.''

The fingers Angie had entwined in his hair stilled, and she ceased her efforts to pull him forward. ''What?'' she asked quietly.

Ethan nodded, avoiding her eyes, focusing, instead, on the soft skin he had bared at her neck. ''Legal,'' he repeated. ''And, uh…and binding. As in me and you are man and wife. Legally. And now that I think about it,'' he added quickly, ''biblically, too.'' When he finally looked up, he forced a strained chuckle and asked, ''How about that? Pretty comical, huh?''

''I thought you said your friend was a *former* man of the

cloth," she said. "That he had *left* the church. That he *wasn't* allowed to preside over weddings."

Ethan nodded a little anxiously. "Yeah, see, that's what *I* thought, too. And he's not allowed to preside over weddings…in the state of Pennsylvania, anyway, because his license *was* revoked there. Turns out, though, that it's perfectly okay for him to marry people in other states. How about that? Funny, huh?"

She let that settle in for a minute, a minute she spent staring at him through slitted eyes.

"It's just the weirdest thing," he continued, his enthusiasm abating some. "There was this total breakdown in communication. He thought I *did* want to get married, and I just assumed he knew I was going for this pseudo kind of marriage, and neither one of us bothered to confirm or…or…" His voice trailed off. "Well, we just misunderstood each other, that's all. Pretty humorous, huh?"

Still Angie wasn't sure what to say, so still she remained silent as she considered him.

"But it's good, too," he rushed on. "Because you know how we forgot to use, um, protection…on our wedding night? This way, if you turn up pregnant, the little guy will be perfectly legit, you know?"

When she still said nothing in response, he dropped his gaze to the mattress, where his fingers seemed to be inordinately interested in smoothing out a wrinkle in the sheet.

"I, uh, I thought you'd be happy to hear that," he said softly. "Seeing as how you might turn up pregnant and all. Seeing as how we love each other and all."

"I'm not pregnant," she told him, suddenly worried about what his response to that might be.

Had he come back to Endicott only because he thought she might be pregnant? she wondered. Was this whole thing just a charade on his part because he was feeling guilty about maybe having left her in a family way? Was he lying about still being in love with her for the sake of a child he may have fathered? And now that he knew he was off the hook, would he swipe a hand over his sweaty brow in relief and say, "Whoa, Angel, just kidding!" as he ran back through the door?

She was surprised to see that his eyes, when he looked up at her again, held disappointment. Sadness, even. And something she had been holding closed tight inside her suddenly burst open wide. What had been an empty hollow surrounded by anxiety and loneliness was suddenly filled with warmth and promise. And Angie was amazed to discover that her love for Ethan had grown even more.

"No one says we can't try again, though," she told him with a tentative smile.

And that, at last, broke the spell. Whatever tension and uncertainty lingered between them evaporated like so much steam. Ethan reached for her, coiling his arms around her, and covered her mouth with his.

"So does this mean you're not gonna file for divorce?" he asked when he pulled away.

"On what grounds?" she replied with a smile.

He shrugged. "Got me."

She nodded. "Yeah, I do got you. And I'm never letting you go."

Before he could confirm or deny her assurance, Angie pulled him toward her again, swiveling his body until she could shove him down onto the mattress and align herself with him.

"You know, you still owe me thirty hours of a honeymoon," she told him. "You promised. You don't want to make a liar out of yourself, do you?"

He smiled as he circled her waist with strong arms. "As far as I'm concerned, Angel, this honeymoon never has to end."

"Okay," she conceded. "That's good enough for me."

She held his gaze steady for a moment, content, for now, to simply absorb him visually. Close to her body, into her heart. Once again, she threaded her fingers through his hair, then she lowered her head to kiss him gently.

"So we really are married?" she asked.

He nodded. "We really are."

"You're never going to leave me again?"

He shook his head. "Never."

"You're staying in Endicott?"

He smiled and scored her hair with his own fingers. "Yeah. I'm staying. I hope you don't mind having an unemployed husband for a while. There's not a lot of call for what I do in this little burg."

"That's true…" she agreed, her voice and her thoughts beginning to trail off.

"Then again," he added with a shrug that was nowhere near careless, "I'm not so sure I want to keep doing what I've been doing."

Angie's preoccupation vanished, her attention focusing on the man who made her feel so warm and wonderful inside. "Why not?" she asked him.

He stroked his hand through her hair and gazed into her eyes, his smile soft and sad. "It's just not that great a gig, you know? Working undercover so much, living that life for so long, adopting the role of low-life, scumbag, murdering slug.…" He sighed, an aching, lonesome sound. "Sometimes you start to feel like one. Sometimes you start to wonder if maybe you're not just like the bad guys after all."

She smiled at him. "You're not one of the bad guys, Ethan. You never were."

He nodded, then kissed each of her cheeks softly. "Yeah, I've been saved by an angel," he told her with a smile. "Too bad she's gonna have to support both of us for a while, though."

Angie's thoughts drifted off again for a moment, and after a moment, she asked, "Ethan?"

He dropped his hands to the backs of her knees and was scooting her nightshirt up over her thighs when he murmured, "Hmm?"

"You said you graduated from Penn State, right?" The nightshirt moved a little higher, and Angie felt the kiss of an autumn breeze dance along her bare legs. She shivered, more from anticipation than the cool air.

"Mmm-hmm," he concurred.

"What, um, what's your degree in?"

"Law enforcement. But I minored in chemistry," he added, sounding very distracted by something. "It's why I was chosen for this particular assignment. Why?"

The hands that had been skimming along the backs of her legs were suddenly cupped over her fanny, and Angie gasped at the hot sensations that rippled through her. She reached down and found the hem of Ethan's sweater, then dipped her hand below it, spreading her fingers wide over the warm, bristly skin she found beneath.

"I was just thinking…" she began, drawing his sweater up higher over his torso.

"Oh, I've been thinking, too," he said, shoving her nightshirt higher still to open his hands over her bare back. "You wouldn't believe what I've been thinking the last week."

Angie chuckled and lifted herself away from him enough to push his sweater up higher. "Take this off," she instructed him.

He laughed. "Yes, ma'am."

"In fact, just take all your clothes off, and I'll tell you about my plan."

"Ooo, Angel, I love it when you talk dirty." He jackknifed eagerly up from the bed and immediately stripped off his sweater.

She followed suit, peeling off her nightshirt as he struggled with his jeans. "That comes later," she told him as she bounced back down on the bed.

He halted his fight with the laces of his hiking boots and gazed hungrily at her bare body. "How much later?"

She lay down on her side, completely naked, one elbow propped beneath her head. "I want to talk to you about my father."

He gaped at her. *"Now?"*

"He needs someone like you."

Ethan straightened, boots still in place, jeans down around his ankles. "Angel, I was kinda hoping *you* needed me."

"Oh, I do," she assured him as the heat of desire raced through her. "But Daddy should have retired years ago. Maybe if he has someone like you working at the company, he can at least go down to part-time." She mimicked his South Philly accent as she added, "You know what I'm sayin' here?"

He grinned and sat back down on the bed, then hastily untied and removed his boots. After peeling off his jeans, he threw himself down on the bed beside Angie. "I'll talk to him Monday morning. Right now, though, I have a honeymoon to finish."

Without further discussion, Angie opened her arms to him, and Ethan fell eagerly into them. He buried his head in her neck, palmed her breasts with his hands and rolled until he covered her body completely with his. Angie bent her knees and arched her pelvis against him, feeling him grow ripe against her belly. Then she cupped his hard buttocks in her hands. He rocked against her, then insinuated his thigh between her legs. She rode him hard as he lowered his head to her breasts, laving her, loving her, savoring her under his tongue.

Angie reached between their bodies to curl her fingers around his avid shaft, and he groaned at her caress. Neither of them pretended that this coupling would be a long, languid, lazy one, and instead turned to each other with anxious need. Ethan rolled to his back and pulled Angie atop him, and she lowered herself over him, damp and hot and ready.

They cried out as one at the lengthy union, then she rose on her knees and lowered herself over him again, slowly, easily, thoroughly. He gripped her hips with strong fingers and urged her to go faster, and she graciously complied with his silent request. He bucked hard against her, and she absorbed him completely, arching her back to increase the friction of their bodies, reaching behind herself to maximize his pleasure.

He moaned and mimicked her gesture, thumbing the soft folds of flesh that lay open to him.

Sensation overcame thought, feeling eclipsed reason, and together they peaked in an explosion of intoxicating need. Then slowly, oh, so slowly, they descended together. Angie fell to the mattress beside Ethan, gasping for breath, panting for oxygen, groping for coherent thought.

Somehow, she found the strength to drape an arm across his damp chest, wanting to hold on to him this way forever. He turned to his side to look at her, one hand cupped over her hip, the other tangling in her hair. His eyes were full of love and longing, something she was certain must be reflected in her own.

"I love you, Ethan," she whispered.

"I love you, too, Angel."

It occurred to her then that Bob may have been the one who brought them together, but it was love that would keep them this way. For better or worse. For richer, for poorer. In sickness and in health. Forever and ever. Till death do them part.

And that, Angie knew, really was a wish come true.

* * * * *

Don't miss the next case of COMET FEVER in
Beauty and the Brain *available in October.*

COMING NEXT MONTH

THE SEDUCTION OF FIONA TALLCHIEF
Cait London

Man of the Month

A Palladin man to marry a Tallchief woman? It was unthinkable—the families were long-burning enemies! But Joel Palladin had watched Fiona Tallchief's fiery beauty from afar and was determined to have her—whatever the cost...

THE PRINCESS BRIDE Diana Palmer

Tiffany Blair vowed to walk down the aisle as Kingman Marshall's bride. King thought marriage was for fools! But he'd give anything to carry sheltered Tiffany over the threshold to womanhood...

THE BABY NOTION Dixie Browning

Daddy Knows Last

Jake Spencer liked the way babies are made—but wasn't planning on making one himself. Until he overheard that the sexiest girl in town was planning a trip to the sperm clinic... Could he convince Priss to do her baby-making the old-fashioned way?

BEAUTY AND THE BRAIN Elizabeth Bevarly

Comet Fever

Be careful what you wish for! Too bad, Rosemary March hadn't heeded this advice fifteen years ago. She'd asked for brainy Willis Random to meet his match, now he had—and it was her!

UNEXPECTED FATHER Kelly Jamison

True, Hannah Brewster had never *told* Jordan McClennon that he was the father of the child she was looking after. But he was busy planning the perfect wedding when Hannah discovered what he suspected—and told him the truth!

A MARRIAGE MADE IN JOEVILLE Anne Eames

Montana Malones

Savannah Smith had changed a great deal since her school days, but she'd never forgotten Ryder Malone. So she decided to go to Joeville to find out if the sexy loner was ready for marriage—and to go in disguise...

COMING NEXT MONTH FROM

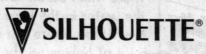 **SILHOUETTE**®

Sensation

A thrilling mix of passion, adventure and drama

SERENA McKEE'S BACK IN TOWN Marie Ferrarella
SAVING SUSANNAH Beverly Bird
HIDE IN PLAIN SIGHT Sara Orwig
THE MAN SHE ALMOST MARRIED Maggie Price

Intrigue

Danger, deception and desire

THE HERO'S SON Amanda Stevens
HER MOTHER'S ARMS Kelsey Roberts
AFTER THE DARK Patricia Rosemoor
WATCH OVER ME Carly Bishop

Special Edition

Satisfying romances packed with emotion

THE NINE-MONTH MARRIAGE Christine Rimmer
THE RANCHER MEETS HIS MATCH Patricia McLinn
WILDCATTER'S KID Penny Richards
TEXAN'S BRIDE Gail Link
THE MAVERICK MARRIAGE Cathy Gillen Thacker
BABY ON HIS DOORSTEP Diana Whitney

There must be something in the water in the little town of New Hope, there are certainly a lot of babies on the way! In this exciting new series, meet five delighted Mums-to-be.

And the handsome hunks who get some surprising news...

Starting next month with:

THE BABY NOTION
Dixie Browning
DESIRE October 1998

Followed by:

BABY IN A BASKET
Helen R. Myers
DESIRE November 1998

MARRIED...WITH TWINS!
Jennifer Mikels
SPECIAL EDITION December 1998

HOW TO HOOK A HUSBAND (AND A BABY)
Carolyn Zane
DESIRE January 1999

DISCOVERED: DADDY
Marilyn Pappano
SENSATION February 1999

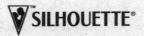

FIND THE FRUIT!

How would you like to win a year's supply of Silhouette® Books—FREE! Well, if you know your fruit, then you're already one step ahead when it comes to completing this competition, because all the answers are fruit! Simply decipher the code to find the names of ten fruit, complete the coupon overleaf and send it to us by 31st March 1999. The first five correct entries will each win a year's subscription to the Silhouette series of their choice. What could be easier?

A	B	C	D	E	F	G	H	I
15					20			
J	K	L	M	N	O	P	Q	R
	25						5	
S	T	U	V	W	X	Y	Z	
			10					

4	19	15	17	22

15	10	3	17	15	18	3

2	19	17	8	15	6	23	2	19

4	19	15	6

4	26	9	1

7	8	6	15	11	16	19	6	6	13

3	6	15	2	21	19

15	4	4	26	19

1	15	2	21	3

16	15	2	15	2	15

C8I

Please turn over for details of how to enter ➜

HOW TO ENTER

There are ten coded words listed overleaf, which when decoded each spell the name of a fruit. There is also a grid which contains each letter of the alphabet and a number has been provided under some of the letters. All you have to do, is complete the grid, by working out which number corresponds with each letter of the alphabet. When you have done this, you will be able to decipher the coded words to discover the names of the ten fruit! As you decipher each code, write the name of the fruit in the space provided, then fill in the coupon below, pop this page into an envelope and post it today. Don't forget you could win a year's supply of Silhouette® Books—you don't even need to pay for a stamp!

Silhouette Find the Fruit Competition
FREEPOST CN81, Croydon, Surrey, CR9 3WZ
EIRE readers: (please affix stamp) PO Box 4546, Dublin 24.

Please tick the series you would like to receive if you
are one of the lucky winners

Desire™ ❏   Special Edition™ ❏   Sensation™ ❏   Intrigue™ ❏

Are you a Reader Service™ subscriber?   Yes ❏   No ❏

Ms/Mrs/Miss/Mr ....Initials ....
                                         (BLOCK CAPITALS PLEASE)
Surname..

Address ....

....

....Postcode.........................

(I am over 18 years of age)   C8I